Becoming A

SARAH ZANE

To my ex husband whose love was conditional, I learned to love myself more than you ever did.

And to everyone else whose success and happiness is just a little spite fueled, this one's for you. If anyone ever tells you writing a revenge fantasy won't make you feel any better, they're lying.

Content Warning

I wanted to put in a brief note here to let you know that there is spice in this book (meaning there are a couple of sex scenes). Since my books normally don't have sex scenes, I wanted to give a warning. I've been told that the spice is between a 2 and a 3 out of 5. Do with that what you will.

And to my family – Read at your own risk.

PROLOGUE

SAVANNAH

I took the stairs two at a time, tears streaming down my face hard enough to obscure my vision. I just needed to get there and everything would be okay. I poured all my energy into making it to safety, telling myself then I could collapse in on myself. Then I could let myself really break. Finally making it to the bottom of the stairs, I turned a corner and yanked open the door to the studio. Pushing it closed, I leaned my back against the door and sunk to the floor, letting out a screaming sob as I fell. My soundproof studio eating up my wails. It was like crying in the shower. Were you really crying if no one was around to hear?

He had seen me start to cry, but I would never let him see me like this. No one ever saw me like this. This was between me and my studio, me and my songs. I only recorded my rawest music in my own studio, where it was just me, myself, and I. It was my happy place. Well, happy place was a stretch, but it was my safe place.

He could have followed me. I ran from him with these tears streaming down my face. He could have come to check on me. He should have, but he didn't follow me. If he loved me, he wouldn't be letting me face this alone. He wouldn't be letting me drown in my grief. I was technically leaving him, but he was leaving me no choice.

More sobs wrenched out of my throat as I tried to catch my breath. I calmed enough that I could see through my tears and picked up my phone. I started to scroll to Lexi to call her but thought better of it. I didn't want anyone to hear me right now, but I needed to talk to someone. I opened up a text and started to type furiously. I finished the third paragraph of my rant before realizing I was humming it. I blinked back the tears, looking at the words I had written to her a little more critically, before pushing myself up, moving across the room, and grabbing my notebook and pen. I was on to something.

Chapter 1

Savannah

Connor's laughter rang out as he barely dodged the pillow I threw at him.

"Do you want my help or not?"

He held up his hands in a placating gesture, made less sincere by the fact that he was still laughing.

"Okay, okay. You're right, but geez Sav, these have to be things I would say."

I looked back at the lyrics I had written down, looking at them more critically and after a moment, had to admit he wasn't wrong.

When I agreed to help him write a love song for his fiancée, I hadn't thought it would be this difficult. I could write lyrics in my sleep. I actually kept a notebook on my nightstand in case inspiration struck in the middle of the night. More than a few times I had abruptly woken from a dream and needed to get my thoughts out. Writing lyrics came easy to me, but helping Connor write them was turning out to be more difficult.

Connor had a good voice, but he much preferred to be in the background. He was my drummer but quickly became like family to me. With him recording with me and touring with me, him, Stevie our guitarist, and I spent more time together than apart. I was so touched he asked for my help.

He was going to serenade his soon-to-be wife on their wedding day while I played the piano accompaniment. She was going to love it, or she would if we could get the lyrics right. I was getting frustrated, and he knew me well enough to know no creative good came from that.

"Snack break?" he asked, already moving toward my kitchen.

A surefire way to get the creativity flowing.

Some strawberries, grapes, cheese, and a couple glasses of wine later, we had a verse and a chorus. It was more progress than we had made for most of the day, though, so it was a victory.

"A toast," he proclaimed.

"To?"

"To us and our bright futures, obviously."

I laughed at that. "Obviously, to you and your happy marriage."

"And to you and your happier divorce."

I had just enough wine in me to laugh heartily at that. He grinned at me, and I grabbed the bottle from him, "I'll drink to that," I said, chugging straight from the bottle. His laughter warmed me as much as the wine did.

"So, how is it living in paradise anyway?"

He smiled shyly. "Things have been really good. I can't wait to marry her already." A shadow fell over his face and he added, "Truth be told, I'm hoping the wedding will stop the Covannah rumors. Emily is getting sick of them and I can't blame her."

I grimaced at that. I loved my fans, I really did but you didn't get to be as famous as I was without some crazy ones and without them pushing your boundaries. Even when Darren and I were happily married, there were rumors floating around that Connor and I were having an affair. The people that shipped us called us Covannah. Before, we were all able to laugh it off, but now that I was separated from Darren, the rumors had gone from an occasional nuisance to unavoidable. As much as he and I denied the rumors, the fans didn't stop, and as much as Connor tried to downplay it to me, I knew Emily was having a harder time with it than he was letting on. Of course she was. She knew there was nothing more than friendship between Connor and me, but it was hard for her having her fiancée in the tabloids. Having to dodge questions from her friends and family and assure them he was faithful. I couldn't imagine how tiring that would get, and as much as I tried to ignore it, I knew something had to give.

I hoped he was right, that the wedding would change things, but if it didn't, I would have to find another way to shut down the rumors.

Chapter 2

The Secret Behind Savannah Hollywood's Latest Hit: Darren Dawson Tells All

Savannah Hollywood has done it again with her latest heartbreaking ballad, taking the world by storm and soaring to the top of the charts.

All over the world, young women are screaming their hearts out to her sorrowful tune. Just what inspired the gut-wrenching lyrics is the source of much talk, but it doesn't take a detective to deduce they have to be about a certain famous soon to be ex-husband of hers.

Savannah herself has yet to confirm or deny that the lyrics are about her upcoming divorce. Both her and Darren have stayed quiet about the whole affair, so to speak. Until now, that is.

For the first time since their very private separation, Darren is speaking out. We sat down with Darren Dawson and have the scoop for you.

Host: Darren, welcome! We're happy to have you. Take a seat, make yourself comfy.

Darren: Thank you, thank you. Pleasure to be here.

Host: We appreciate you taking the time from your busy schedule with your upcoming movie.

Darren: Yes, that's right. A Night to Remember has kept me quite busy, but I'm always happy to take the time to give the people what they want.

Darren winked at the camera playfully.

Host: And boy do they want it.

The host grinned conspiratorially at Darren before turning back to the camera.

Host: Everyone has been speculating and wondering, but today, here and now, we're going to get some answers.

Darren turned to the camera, too, nodding solemnly.

Darren: That's right. I figured it was finally time I told my truth, since Savannah hasn't been quiet about hers.

Host: You mean in her songs?

Darren: Yes, her songs. We agreed to keep everything private. I didn't tell anyone what she did to me. Even after everything she put me through, I chose to take the high ground, but clearly I was the only one who did and I'm sick of covering for her.

The host looked at the camera with barely contained glee.

Host: So, you're saying there's more to the story?

Darren: Absolutely! I'm saying there's a whole lot more to the story than that bullshit song she wrote about me tearing her apart, or ripping out her heart, or some bullshit like that.

The host's grin lit up the studio, but he took a moment to remind Darren,

Host: I know this is emotional, but we have to try to keep it PG for the viewers at home.

Darren looked ashamed and quickly said,

Darren: I know. I'm sorry. It's just still so hard to talk about.

Darren sniffled before reaching into his pocket and taking out a handkerchief and dabbing his eyes.

Host: It's okay, take your time.

Darren dabbed his eyes a couple of times each before swallowing and nodding.

Darren: Okay, I think I'm ready.

Host: And we're here for you. Myself and everyone at home are dying to hear what really happened, dying to hear from you.

Darren: Well, I can tell you that song is undoubtably about me, but things didn't go down like that. She stole the lyrics from me.

The host blinked, shocked, before blurting out,

Host: You can't mean...?

Darren: I do. She broke my heart, ripping it right in two, and it killed me watching her leave. She took the better parts of me, leaving me empty. God knows it didn't take her long to move on, either.

Host: Wait, wait, wait.

The host looked at the camera, grinning ear to ear.

Host: Don't worry, everyone, we'll circle back to that, but going back for a second, are you saying you wrote the song?

Darren: I might as well have. She technically wrote it, but I gave her the material, the thoughts, the pain, the words. Those were things I told her when she was leaving. She wrote it from my point of view. She broke me, and then used my heartbreak, my pain, to write her song. She put out this false narrative that she did everything to try to get me to stay when that couldn't be further from the truth. I did everything to try to keep her, to save our marriage, but she had already checked out. No one can say that girl doesn't move on quick.

Host: Wait, does that mean she's seeing someone?

Darren: Several someones. I'm not sure which one was the reason she left me, but she hadn't been faithful for a long time.

Darren paused a moment, considering, before shaking his head.

Darren: Actually, that's not true. I don't know why, even now, I feel like I should be protecting her. I know why she left me. I know his name, and yet here I am, still shielding her, still protecting her.

Darren took a long pause, causing the Host to ask,
Host: Why?

Darren: I guess I've always been chivalrous, but the real reason is so much worse. I'm protecting her because as terrible as she's been, as embarrassing as it is,

I'm still unfortunately in love with her. I never wanted to hurt her, but I'm getting sick of protecting her, of letting her paint me as the bad guy.

Host: Well, you have a chance to clear that up.

Darren: The drummer.

Host: What about a drummer?

Darren: The drummer in her band, that's who she was fucking towards the end of our marriage.

The live audience gasped, and then immediately started BOOing. The Host tried to quiet them down, but the audience was in an uproar.

Savannah

I grabbed the remote from Lexi's hand and turned off the TV. I had seen enough.

"That lying son of a bitch," I swore. "What the hell did I just watch?"

"Tell me about it," she groaned. "It's going to take a lot to get out of this one, even for me."

Lexi was my manager, but she was so much more than that. She was also my lawyer, sometimes acted as my publicist and agent, and my best friend all wrapped into one. Not only that, since the split with Darren, she had been my rock. I wasn't close with my family and losing Darren and the family I had married into all at the same time had hit me hard. It was clearer than ever that Lexi was the only one I could depend on. Well, her and my band of course. I looked over at Lexi and saw her anger mirrored my own.

She had the same shade of blonde hair I did and her eyes were a paler blue than mine, but we frequently were mistaken for sisters. Seeing her face twisted into disgust, anger, and concern, I knew I should have been worried. As a best friend, she was the best, but as a manager and a lawyer, she was even better. She was the best in the business.

She really knew what she was doing, so if she was worried, I was terrified. She had dug celebrities out of holes so deep they should have drowned and brought them back into the spotlight. She had single-handedly saved and ruined careers. She was the best, and I shuddered to think about where I would be without her in my corner.

"But we will, right? You have a plan?"

She looked thoughtful for a moment before nodding slowly. "I do, but I know you're not going to like it."

I gulped.

We had been working together for three years, ever since I started making enough to afford having her on my payroll, and we became fast friends. She quickly became one of the most important people in my life.

It had disappointed me that, from the jump, she had always hated Darren. She was such a good judge of character, so I didn't understand why she didn't like him. I should have taken that more seriously, but he fooled me, blinded me like he had apparently done to so many other women.

After he left me, Lexi started doing some digging, and after the first couple of women, I told her to stop. I couldn't handle hearing about the parade of affairs he had, but I knew she was still uncovering them, doing her job. She knew we were going to need as much evidence as possible for the divorce trial. She was preparing me that he was going to come after me hard and she wanted to take everything from him. He had so much debt that it wouldn't be hard to do. As Lexi put it, he hadn't booked a good-paying job in a while and was clinging to relevance, using me as a life raft.

She expected him to try to squeeze as much from me as he could, and she didn't want him to get a dime. Had he been worth much of anything, I'm sure she would have wanted to take him for all he was worth, but he didn't have much to his name.

I just wanted this to be over with. I wanted out, quickly. She wanted revenge.

I hadn't believed her when we first separated and she started trying to prepare me for how badly this could go. Why would I have? He cheated on me. Surely there wasn't a way he could spin that to make people sympathetic to him, but having just watched his interview, clearly I was wrong. He was a lying bastard, and she was right to be worried.

I could see the 'I told you so' on her face, but she didn't say it. She had warned me about his retaliation when I played her the song, but I thought she was worried about nothing. The song came from my heart and I wanted to put it out into the world. I had no idea how big of a can of worms I was opening, but the song was out there now and there was no taking it back.

With how quickly he jumped to do the media circuits after the song released, I had to assume he had been planning for this.

What I couldn't believe and what was pissing me off even more than him blatantly lying about my 'affairs' that never happened was that he dragged Connor into this. Darren knew how much Emily struggled with the rumors about me and Connor, and I couldn't believe he would stoop low enough to add fuel to the fire.

It was a lower blow with more collateral damage than I expected from him. He knew how much Emily struggled with Connor's job, with him leaving for long periods of time to tour with me. This would make his and her lives so much worse. With him confirming it, the fans were never going to stop and the reporters were going to harass Connor and Emily more than they already did.

"Normally, I would recommend using Connor as a whirlwind romance, playing into the rumors and showing people that Connor saved you from the abuse."

"Not an option." I said, cutting her off. I wouldn't ask any more of him and Emily.

She waved her hand quickly, dismissing it. "I know, I know. I wasn't even going to recommend it. I just wanted you to know how deep in shit we are right now. That would be my usual way out, but I think you're going to like my other suggestion even less."

"There's no way. Anything that gets Connor out of the equation would have to be better than that."

"Okay, but don't say I didn't warn you."

I gulped. This was going to be bad.

Chapter 3

Savannah

"You want me to do what?" I asked, not quite believing my ears.

"I don't want you to. Believe me, I don't and if there were any other way, I would, but you ruled out my only other plan," Lexi pleaded, frustration and concern warring on her face.

"Because it wasn't an option."

"Which is fine, but if that isn't, this is the only other option we have."

"You can't be serious, though. You want me to come out to the public and hire someone to parade around as my girlfriend?"

"Only if you're ready to come out. If you're not, we can hire someone to parade around as your boyfriend. Although I do think the public would like the queer angle better, and on a personal note, you taking a break from men wouldn't be the worst thing."

She wasn't wrong. If I was going to fake date someone, I would prefer it to be a woman, but that would mean coming out. Not that I was hiding my sexuality, but I had been married to Darren and hadn't exactly been loud about it.

"Okay, fine."

She grinned. "A woman?"

I nodded.

"Perfect! I can spin the hell out of this; Darren and that no-good stuck-up lawyer who thinks he's better than everyone won't know what hit them."

"Wait a second, you forgot to clue me in on the kind of important detail. Who are you hiring?"

She looked sheepish before saying, "Well, you remember me telling you about the company I used to find a nanny for that rich former client whose wife passed away?" The confusion was clear on my face, because she kept going, "The one who didn't trust anyone around his kids? Who had a ridiculous list of demands no sane person would have agreed to?"

"Vaguely, but what do they have to do with..." I trailed off right as I realized where she was going with this. "You want me to trust the future of my career, of my life, to some stranger some random company is going to hire? Would they even do that? A fake girlfriend is a bit of a stretch from a nanny."

"I know from dealing with them there isn't much they won't do, and they aren't some random company. Elite is the best of the best."

"Yes, because no other company does what they do!"

"For good reason, no one else could."

"No one else would. It's insane. Hiring someone to pretend to be my girlfriend is insane."

She grinned, making me nervous. "Well, there's one other option we have."

I waited, but she didn't continue. I felt the hope rise up a little as I asked, "Which is?"

She nudged me with her shoulder. "You could go out and get a real girlfriend."

I rolled my eyes. She knew I wasn't about to start dating anyone anytime soon despite her continued encouragement to put myself back out there.

"So, what'll it be? Should I make the call, or are you going to find yourself a date?"

I glared at her and said quietly, "Make the call."

"What? I didn't hear you."

"Make the call," I grumbled louder.

"So, what you're saying is...?"

I groaned. "What I'm saying is you're a pain in my ass."

She grinned. "But..."

"But you're the best and, once again, you're right."

As she stepped out to make the call, I had to stop myself from calling her back, already regretting my decision.

I had wanted to go public about Darren's affairs and let the chips fall where they may, I believed that my fans would be on my side, but Lexi wasn't willing to bet my divorce case or career on it. She told me that even if people believed me, which was a big if, it would let Darren know what we were planning with the divorce case.

He was angling for alimony and half my assets. We had a prenup of course, but it had been drawn up by his lawyers. He had insisted we both needed the protection, just in case, and like a fool in love I had trusted him.

I didn't even have a lawyer of my own look it over. Lexi wasn't in my life at that point, but I could have had someone, anyone else that wasn't on his payroll look it over, but I didn't. Lexi hadn't been able to get a copy of the document yet, so she was anxious about what we were walking into it.

Right now, his infidelity was her ace up the sleeve to trump whatever his team might be cooking up. As much as it frustrated me, she was right. Right now, he thought I was giving in and letting him control the narrative, willing to give him what he wanted. We had the advantage, and we needed to keep it. Especially with Darren's counsel being who he was.

Darren hiring Jared Davidson was just another reason Lexi was determined to bury him. Being on Lexi's bad side was a terrible place to be, but she had an especially strong hatred for Jared ever since he beat her out for college valedictorian. She still claims to this day he rigged the system to get back at her for beating the pants off him in their final debate team tournament. She was even more serious about beating him and Darren than I was, so as she had put it "revealing our hand to the enemy before we have to is not an option."

So, it looked like we were really doing this. I was going to be taking on the role of a lifetime, faking a relationship.

I was nauseous just thinking about it. I got up from the couch and went to the kitchen. A warm cup of tea might not solve all my problems, but it was just what I needed right now.

I could see through the glass sliding door that Lexi was pacing around on the porch, still on the phone, but some of the anxiety calmed when she turned and I saw she looked excited.

She saw me watching and gave me a thumbs up. I forced a smile back hoping she was right about this.

THE BI-CON PROJECT

The Client: Savannah Hollywood

Age: 30

Location: Beverly Hills, California

Current occupation: Singer/popstar

The problem: Savannah is about to be going through a highly publicized divorce with current husband Darren Dawson, a highly popular actor. Darren has been telling the press that Savannah cheated on him with her drummer and Savannah's team needs that story to get buried. They also want positive publicity surrounding Savannah since her newest album release is coming up and they don't want her career to suffer because of her divorce.

The client's suggestion: Savannah's team recommended a fake girlfriend would give the press something new to talk about. Savannah's team say she identifies as bisexual and would be willing to come out to make this plan work.

Elite's verdict: With some modifications to her plan and careful hiring, getting Savannah a fake girlfriend would work to distract from the divorce and control the narrative. In order for this to work and go off without a hitch, very careful planning must be implemented. We will need to know everything there is to know about Savannah Hollywood to take her from icon to bi-con. IF we undertake this, from here on out, it will be referred to as the bi-con project.

The Next Steps:

-    Dig up everything possible on Savannah Hollywood. We need to know everything and anything there is to know about her. Anything that may or may not be relevant, we don't want any surprises. This won't go sideways like last time.

-    Have her take the

o Myers Briggs personality test

o Love Languages test

o Fight Languages test

o DOPE bird personality test

-    Calculate her zodiac sun, moon, and rising

-    Pull our currently available contact files, looking for a woman

o Mid 20s to late 30s

o Preferably queer passing, if not actually queer

o Preferably some experience with being in the public eye

o Someone good at acting and comfortable lying

Deadline: Savannah's team needs an answer and if yes, for our team to start in a week.

Priority: Urgent

CHAPTER 4

SAVANNAH

It turns out hiring a fake girlfriend isn't as easy as simply being able to afford it. Elite doesn't take on just any client, but they were already taking the potential job way more seriously than I expected. When they told us they needed a week to consider and strategize before deciding if it was a job they could take on, I had assumed that meant we wouldn't hear from them until they had decided. Boy was I wrong.

Lexi had been filling out a bunch of paperwork about my life and our requirements for the candidate, while I had been kept busy with enough personality tests that I was starting to wonder if Elite was sponsored by BuzzFeed. I was familiar with a couple of the ones they had me take, but some were new to me.

I hadn't even heard of the DOPE bird test before. It sorted you into types of birds between a dove, owl, peacock and eagle. The dove was introverted and emotion driven, the owl introverted and goal driven, the peacock extroverted and emotion driven, and lastly the eagle was extroverted and goal driven. I had thought I was going to be a dove, but ended up being sorted into peacock. It was funny, I knew I was able to act extroverted, you had to for my job, but I never would have said I was actually extroverted. Although the peacock with its flashy feathers wasn't too far off from my flashier concert costumes.

I supposed the tests weren't the worst thing in the world, but I couldn't imagine how knowing I was a peacock was going to be even remotely helpful to Elite. Even ignoring the DOPE bird test, they were a lot more focused on compatibility than I had expected. It felt like what I imagined a real matchmaking service would do, especially since they had me figure out my love language and fighting style in arguments. It was like they thought there had to be compatibility in order for us to pull this off. It was a smart way to approach it, I'd give them that. The next two months would be much easier if I was compatible with the person.

Not that it mattered how compatible we were, I wasn't looking to date anyway, no matter how compatible we were. I really hoped Elite would come through for me, because I had no idea what we would do without them.

AMERICA'S SWEETHEART FALLS FROM GRACE

Savannah Hollywood and Darren Dawson are well on their way to the most talked about divorce Hollywood has seen in a long time. We never thought these lovebirds would split and while it pains us to report they have, we know you want all the juicy details.

An anonymous source close to the couple confirmed Darren caught Savannah with her drummer Connor in a compromising position. How could America's Sweetheart could be so cruel? How will Darren recover and move on?

The anonymous source disclosed that Darren is still healing, but that this didn't make him stop believing in love. He now knows he just has to be more careful with his heart. That's right ladies, Darren Dawson is single again and might be looking for love sooner rather than later. Savannah Hollywood's loss is our gain.

DAWLLYWOOD WALKED SO COVANNAH COULD RUN

Savannah Hollywood has finally done what her true fans have been begging her to do for ages, left her cruel husband for her drummer, Connor. Connor has been pining after her for years, not that anyone from Hollywood's team would admit that, but we aren't blind. The way he watches her when she sings, the way he follows her every move when they perform made it clear he wanted her. She wasn't subtle either with her soft smiles to him and the way she looks back at him when she's performing.

Her true fans knew there was no way it was strictly professional between those two .Anyone with eyes has been shipping them from the jump, and anyone who knows Savannah at all knows she has nothing in common with her jerk of a husband. If it wasn't for him, she would be touring more and making more music, instead, he had her stifled. Anyone who knows her knows he was just holding her back. It was clear he was jealous of her fame, and now she's skyrocketed and he's still making mediocre movies, he couldn't stand it.

I wasn't at all surprised things didn't work out with them. With how unsupportive he was, no wonder she's with Connor now. That's the only good thing Darren Dawson ever did for her, send her running into Connor's waiting, caring, strong arms.

THE DAWLLYWOOD DIVORCE

We have been waiting and waiting for any updates or developments in what is shaking up to be the most anticipated divorce Hollywood has seen in ages, but there haven't been any updates on just when Dawllywood will have their day in court.

Darren has been doing a lot of interviews about his feelings on the divorce and how heartbroken he is, but he hasn't spoken about the divorce case itself or how he feels that will go. We reached out to his team who declined to comment. We can't help but wonder if they're worried the case might not go their way.

Savannah has been radio silent, or should we say silent on all but the radio. She hasn't said anything explicitly about the divorce, but her songs say a lot for her. If she's to be believed, she was the one heartbroken from the split. Her team wasn't available to comment either, although it's important to note that she's been seen meeting with her lawyer a lot more frequently lately. Could that mean they hope to end this quickly? If so, good luck. It seems like Dawson isn't ready to let things end quite so soon if his interviews are anything to go by.

THE BI-CON PROJECT

Potential Matches:

~~Elise Connolly~~ – too shy

~~Stella Doherty~~ – uncomfortable lying

Maya Ryder

~~Isabelle Woods~~ – bad actress

~~Hannah Wright~~ – too straight, actually straight and too straight looking and not willing to alter appearance

POTENTIAL MATCH #3

Maya Ryder

Age: 30

Location: La Puente, California

Relationship Status: Single

Gender: Female

Sexuality: Lesbian

Status: Available for work

Myers Briggs type: ENTJ

Love Language: Physical touch

Fight Language: Ignitor

DOPE bird type: Eagle

Zodiac signs: Scorpio sun, Leo moon, Taurus rising

Typecast: 20 to 30 something leftist lesbian, pop punk/grunge look, could pass as a drummer in an indie band

Preferred jobs: performing, anything that involves acting or a spotlight, wants to be seen and get her name back out there

Past experience: was a teenage actress on show that required her to act and sing, somewhat popular, might still be recognizable

Any past interactions with the client: Savannah was on the same show with her as a teenager, according to the tabloids, they didn't part on good terms, Savannah left the show to move on to bigger and better things, Maya didn't continue to rise in the industry and had to take odd jobs, and landed on our roster

Requirements if chosen: If away from home for longer than a couple of days, a nurse and home health aid will be needed for her grandmother, of whom she's the regular caregiver.

Pros: She fits the right age range and look as a 30-year-old lesbian who is obviously queer looking. She has a past in the industry and enjoys the spotlight. She has an acting background and is good at it

Cons: Their personalities aren't exactly screaming compatible, their zodiac signs and fight styles show their volatility together. They would either be thick as thieves or want to kill each other

Unknowns: Their past together. If the tabloids can be believed they were the best of friends until the show ended and things turned ugly, we're currently unsure if they've had any contact since or reconciled.

Risks: Highly possible the two of them would do nothing but fight and be at each other's throats, especially because of their shared history.

Rewards: If the women are able to be professional, it would make for a very convincing relationship and big headlines for the press. A second chance romance, estranged best friends turned lovers, old costars sparking a new romance, it would be tabloid gold if they could pull it off.

COMPATIBILITY ANALYSIS

Myers Briggs Types

Savannah: ESFP – extraverted, passionate, empathetic

Maya: ENTJ – extraverted, intelligent, ambitious

Compatibility: They are both extraverted which is a positive, if their goals and priorities align, this pairing could be unstoppable with Maya's ambition and Savannah's passion. If not aligned, it would be a disaster with Maya's ambition and judgment clouding her ability to empathize and Savannah's passion and empathy clouding her ambition.

Love Languages

Savannah: Quality Time

Maya: Physical Touch

Compatibility: Highly compatible assuming Savannah isn't averse to being touched and Maya is able to put aside her ambitious nature to slow down and spend quality time with Savannah

Fight Languages

Savannah: Amplifier – quick to be emotionally overwhelmed

Maya: Ignitor – quick to anger

Compatibility: Not ideal, arguments are likely to quickly escalate into yelling if intervention isn't made. If Maya is chosen, this will have to be addressed and worked on during the training period. They will need to be provided with the signs of when a fight is too escalated and how to cope and deescalate.

DOPE bird types

Savannah: Peacock – extraverted, emotional, showy

Maya: Eagle – extraverted, goal-oriented, leader

Compatibility: Neutral, if they are working toward the same goal, the pairing would be unstoppable. If they're competing for the same goal/spotlight, they might kill each other. If we go with Maya, we will need to make sure to ramp up the teambuilding in training.

Zodiac breakdowns

Savannah

Sun: Leo

Moon: Taurus

Rising: Cancer

Maya
Sun: Scorpio
Moon: Leo
Rising: Taurus

Compatibility:
The Scorpio/Leo pairing is a fiery one, either very good or very bad. They are both passionate and could be prone to power struggles in the relationship if mutual respect isn't established early on

The Taurus/Leo moon pairing is a bit more balanced, both are very loyal, Savannah's stable Taurus could balance out Maya's more fiery Leo in the right circumstances.

The Cancer/Taurus rising pairing also shows some balance between Savannah's emotional cancer and Maya's dependable Taurus. If given the right motivation Maya could balance out Savannah and give her the emotional support she needs.

Compatibility Conclusion: Putting Savannah and Maya together is a high risk, high reward situation. If it works, it will work well. Together, they will be fiery and passionate, whether that's a good thing or a bad thing is up to them. Our team would need to work hard with them in training to help ensure they are working together for their common goal. The key to getting this to work is showing Savannah and Maya that they are on the same team and that by helping each other, they are also helping themselves. If we can get them to see eye to eye and see how mutually beneficial the situation is, this pairing would be ideal. The press would have the story of a lifetime with this Hollywood High Reunion love story.

CHAPTER 5

MAYA

I groaned when my phone rang out, I had meant to put it back on vibrate. It almost always used to be on vibrate, but with my grandma sick, nowadays I left the ringer on, praying it didn't ring, that no one needed me. Right now, though, sitting beside my gram watching Wheel of Fortune with her cat Sunny curled up between us, I knew whatever it was could wait.

I let the phone go to voicemail without looking. If it was important enough, they would call back. The thought barely had time to form before the phone was ringing again.

"Sweetheart, you might want to answer that."

"Can you see the future now?" I asked sweetly before adding, "actually definitely not, you'd be better at Wheel of Fortune if you could." She smacked me lightly and I laughed, "Okay, okay," I said and grabbed the phone. She was reaching for the remote, but I moved instead. "I'll only be a minute, just gonna tell them to leave me alone, you're not winning this round."

She grinned at that, "you're quick as a whip, and sharp as one too."

I couldn't hide my grin and was stifling a laugh when I answered.

"Hello?"

"Hello, is this Maya Ryder?"

"Possibly, depends who's asking."

"I'm calling from Elite Connections, but I'm afraid I can't say anymore until you confirm you're Maya."

"Elite Connections?!" I nearly shouted into the phone. I winced imagining how loud that would have been on the other line. Gram waved at me and mouthed "Elite?" I held up a hand motioning her to wait a moment and said, "I'm so sorry, but is this really Elite?"

"Are you really Ms. Ryder?"

"Yes I am."

"Zodiac sign?"

"Really?" I asked, incredulously.

"Yes, maybe Ms. Ryder. We don't make many offers and we require our candidates to follow instructions well. Is that going to be a problem?"

I could hear the annoyance in her voice and rushed to say "Of course not."

I wasn't an idiot. I needed Elite much more than they needed me. If I didn't do what they needed, I was sure they had plenty of people lined up to take whatever they were going to offer me. There wasn't much known about Elite, just that if they called, you were normally set for life. They were the lottery of Hollywood. A concierge service to the stars, their clients paid life changing amounts of money for their needs to be met. My mind raced through the possibilities, wondering what kind of job they had me in mind for.

I hoped it was something good but one look at my wide-eyed hopeful Gram on the couch made me sure I would take whatever it was. Whatever it was, it would be enough to help make Gram comfortable and help take care of my little sister Leslie and her daughter so she didn't have to work herself quite as hard.

Leslie got divorced last year and was doing everything she could to support and provide for her daughter while also trying to help me with Gram. Gram raised us after our mother died when we were really young and more than anything I wanted to be able to care for her now, but money was tight and it wasn't easy. This could change everything; *Elite* could change everything.

"Zodiacs, sun, moon and rising if you please."

I thought for a moment before answering, "Scorpio sun, Leo moon, Taurus rising."

"Hello, Ms. Ryder."

"Hi there, mysterious Elite employee. What can I do for you?"

"I'm calling to talk about what we can do for you."

Twenty minutes later, I had all but agreed to give my life away and collapsed on the couch with Gram, who looked at me expectantly. When I didn't say anything, she said, "Well get on with it sweetie. Who was that? What did they want?"

"I got a job?" I half stated, half asked. This still didn't feel real. "I can't say much, but if this works out, we're going to be set for a long time." I looked at her then, excitement and guilt rising as I took both her hands in mine. "The numbers they were talking, the money, is an amount I never even dreamed of ever seeing. They're the big leagues, but it would mean me being gone for a little while."

She squeezed my hands and asked, "How long?"

"Two months," I said but rushed to add, "but as long as I'm gone, the company agreed to bring on a private home health aide for you, and…. Wait for it-" I said drumming on my knees for dramatic effect.

"Get on with it, girl, I'm not getting any younger."

I laughed at that and stopped my drumming, "a private chef."

She grinned at that. Gram loved baking but cooking was the bane of her existence, as good as she was at it. "You know, I could certainly get used to that idea," she said, before looking at me and saying "but please don't feel like you need to take care of me. I want what's best for you. Is this job a good one?"

I thought about that a moment. I didn't know too much about it, just that I would spend a couple months getting cozy with a Hollywood hotshot who was coming out and needed a girlfriend. I wondered which Hollywood hottie I would get to date, wondered who was secretly in the closet. I was excited to find out, and really hoped they were a decent person, otherwise the two months would crawl by.

Elite had promised a mansion stay for me, a ton of free publicity, more money than I had ever seen in my life and that they would provide for my Gram while I was gone. They even agreed to amend their "no phones in the first couple weeks" rule to allow for check ins with Gram. I wasn't going otherwise and the way they caved immediately, I was starting to wonder if I actually had more power than I thought, but I knew better than to push my luck. Besides the offer was more than generous already.

"From what I know, I think so. I'm not sure who the woman is I'll be working with, but I do know there's going to be a ton of free publicity baked into the deal."

She smiled at that and I was grateful she didn't say what we were both thinking, how badly I needed the publicity.

I hadn't booked an acting job in months, a noteworthy job in even longer. If this dry spell continued, I was going to have to look for other work to continue to help my Gram and Leslie and my little niece. I couldn't let any of them down. My acting career was on its last leg, and Elite's plan might be just the thing to revive it.

CHAPTER 6

SAVANNAH

There was no way in hell this was my reality. If this was Lexi's idea of a joke, I wasn't laughing and she wouldn't be either when I gave her a piece of my mind. If she were anyone else, I would have fired her on the spot, but she and I both knew I would never do that. I would be lost without her, but she was still going to get an earful about this. I held my breath, waiting for the just kidding, waiting for this to be a joke, a bad dream, anything but reality.

"No," was all I could muster.

Lexi looked at me with genuine surprise. "No? What do you mean, no?"

She had to know. There was no way in hell she didn't know what the rest of the world did. She was the best in the business. The odds that she didn't do her home-work on me before taking the job were slim to none. The odds that she didn't know exactly why the person standing in front of me was, Darren notwithstanding, the last person I would have wanted to see again, were slim to none.

"I mean no. Not her. Anyone else; literally pick someone up off the street if you have to, but not her."

Lexi looked confused and turned to look at the woman standing in front of us. I tried not to look at her but I couldn't help myself. Her hair didn't fall in her trademark raven waves anymore. She had a tall faux-hawk streaked through with different shades of purple. The other side of her head was done up in tiny braids, making it look shaved. Her ears were lined with silver jewelry and her eyebrow was shaved. Even her nose was pierced. She was a far cry from the girl I knew back from our Hollywood High days. More grown up, more punk, more queer, but it was still her.

She was still the Maya I used to share everything with. The girl who was there for me when the rest of the world wasn't. The same Maya I worked with on Hollywood High. The reason I loved going to work and getting to leave, especially when it meant going home with her, getting to spend time with her and her sister, and be around her grandma. They all made me feel so welcome, like I was a part of the family, and I loved it. I loved her family, but she was my everything, or she used to be. Now here she was, standing in front of me, familiar, but nothing was the same.

Her brown eyes were narrowed at me and there was a familiar scowl on her face, but it did nothing to detract from her beauty. With her standing in front of me and my traitorous heart doing flips, I was struggling to remind myself this wasn't the same girl that had been my best friend. This was the girl who had turned on me at the drop of a hat. I knew that, but seeing her in front of me, it was hard to remember. It had been 13 years since the last time I had seen her, but it still felt like yesterday.

"Really?" Lexi asked, scrutinizing me and then the woman before looking back at me. "I know she's no trophy, but I'm sure she's good enough for a couple months, then when she breaks your heart, you can easily find better."

"What?" I blurted out, while she said, "Hey!"

Lexi shot her a look that silenced the woman and said to her, "You're not being paid for your opinions."

I was surprised by the bite in her tone. It wasn't like Lexi. She was usually more tactful than that. If she was snapping at her, maybe she knew. But she couldn't have. She wouldn't have put me in this situation if she knew, right? If she knew, she had to also know that I would have done literally anything else to avoid this. *Well,* I thought for a second, *not literally anything else.* I hadn't been willing to drag Connor into it. She had said Connor was her first choice. If she wasn't my best friend, I would think this was her idea of punishing me for not listening to her, but I knew her better.

I told her to find me another way, any other way, and she did. I should have been more specific.

Even still, I couldn't believe how blatantly rude Lexi was being to her. Then again, I wasn't doing much better. I had hardly said a word to her, hardly looked at her. What was wild to me was that she was still here. That she thought for a second that this was a good idea. From the look of shock on her face, I knew they hadn't told her it would be me. She wouldn't have come if they had, and yet, she was still standing there.

I wasn't sure if she was as paralyzed as I was. Maybe she was going to make a run for it, but one second passed and then another and she hadn't moved. She couldn't possibly think this was a good idea, and besides that, after she turned on me, she couldn't possibly think I would go along with this, did she?

Before I could stop myself, I said, "It's not her looks, it's *her*. What the hell are you doing here, Maya?"

"Trust me, I'm not much happier about it than you are. They promised me an easy gig, two months with America's sweetheart for a mansion stay, free publicity, and more money than I could count for my silence. Knowing it's you, I'm thinking I didn't ask for enough."

Apparently, some things never changed.

Even back then, she never did anything that didn't serve her.

How the hell she had ended up here, though, was a mystery.

"You didn't know?" I asked again.

She rolled her eyes. "Look, Hollywood, I know you're still stuck up enough to think the world revolves around you, but if I had known you were the star that needed help, I would've told Elite to take a hike."

I couldn't do this. I looked at Lexi, panicking. "You have to call them."

Maya sneered at me. "Yeah, call them, tell them little miss perfect over here can't handle any competition. Tell them she's afraid I'll steal the spotlight."

Lexi looked back and forth between us and saw the unbridled panic on my face. She nodded in resignment before pulling out her phone. "I'll see what I can do."

She would fix this. She had to.

"That desperate to get rid of me? I'm not surprised. Wouldn't want your dirty little secrets to come out."

"More like I don't think you're up for the role," I lied. She was good enough for any role; it was me I was worried about.

She glared at me. "You know between the two of us I've always been the better actress."

She didn't have to remind me. She sure had me fooled back then into thinking she cared, that we were actually friends, but I wasn't gullible anymore. I wouldn't be fooled by her again.

When I didn't argue, she got cocky and added, "And singer."

That was one comment too many.

"Clearly. That's why I'm the one on stage."

It was a low blow, but I couldn't help myself. It was a sore subject for me. A few years after having a solo singing career, I started thinking about breaking back into acting. That was around the time I met Darren. Back then he was a handsome movie star who swept me off my feet.

He was good to me and treated me well. I fell for him *hard.* I trusted him, so when he laughed at me when I told him I wanted to act again, I stopped believing in myself as much. He always told me I wasn't good enough to break into serious acting, so after a couple of failed auditions I botched by being too nervous, I started to believe him.

He told me to leave acting to the professionals and stick to what I was good at. I listened back then, but now it pissed me off that I let him make me feel less than for even a moment. I had promised myself I would never let anyone make me feel like that again, and I wasn't about to let Maya make me break that promise. Seeing her was bringing out the worst in me, though, like we were teenagers again.

"You know why you're there and it isn't your talent, at least not your talent for singing," Maya bit out.

I tried to ignore the pang in my chest at that, but that was low even for her. When I broke out into my solo singing career, there were whispers and rumors that I blew up too quickly. When you were propelled to fame like I had been, there would always be people jealous enough to try to tear you down. People used to say I must have slept my way to the top. I just had never expected my best friend would agree with them.

Ex best friend, I reminded myself.

Having that thrown in my face by the person I used to trust with all my secrets had me seeing red.

Lexi re-entered and I swallowed my words, both grateful and annoyed at the interruption. She saved me from saying something I wouldn't have, but probably should have, regretted.

"No luck, Sav. Looks like everyone else is booked."

"No one else wanted the job is more like it," Maya said icily. "No wonder they didn't tell me who the client was. I should've known it was too good to be true."

I should have, too.

I should have been much more specific with Lexi about what I was and wasn't willing to do. Keeping Connor out of the limelight was worth going through hell for, but this was making a deal with the devil herself, and I didn't know how I would manage to get out unscathed.

I didn't believe for a second that even if we somehow pulled off a miracle and got people to believe this, that Lexi wouldn't turn around and sell me out, sell all my secrets to the highest bidder. She wasn't loyal to me then, and she wouldn't be now.

CHAPTER 7

SAVANNAH

Maya's presence was throwing me through a loop, but if I was being honest, it wasn't just Maya that had my head spinning. Even before seeing Elite's choice in women, I had been having my doubts. I had certainly never come close to publicly dating a woman, and I had worried all week since Lexi called Elite about whether I could handle the attention. Now that I was publicly going through a divorce, the press speculated hourly on which new man I was dating if I so much as looked at someone for longer than a moment.

The tabloids continually ran pieces about me dating the waiter at my favorite restaurant because he waited on my table twice in one month. According to the press, any man I sat next to in public or made eye contact with for more than two seconds, I was automatically dating. I didn't know how things would change if I came out, but I imagined they would get worse.

Instead of just speculating on which *guys* I could be dating, now no one would be safe. I wouldn't be able to leave my house, although that wasn't much different from now, if I was being honest.

Coming out would make things unequivocally worse. Stepping into the role of a "bi-con", as Lexi said Elite was calling it, would change my life forever, and I wasn't sure I was ready for the scrutiny. I would have to be, though, because I knew it wasn't just about me, or really even about Connor. Well, I was doing this for Connor, but it would help more than just him. It was also about the representation and what I could do for the LGBTQ+ community. It was about the power I held with the platform I was lucky enough to have, so I agreed. That and I didn't want to be intimately around another man so soon after things had gone sideways with my marriage.

So, Lexi had worked out everything with Elite. Even then, it had sounded too good to be true. A gorgeous woman would move in and be paid to act as my girlfriend and then, in a couple months, she would publicly break my heart. I didn't love the idea of going through another public breakup, but this would be different. This time I was controlling the narrative. The idea was that the public breakup would get me enough sympathy to improve my reputation and get the press to stop speculating about who I was dating, for a while at least.

Truthfully, I was still stunned that Elite was able to set me up with a fake girlfriend. It seemed so far out of the realm of what should have been possible to pay for, but that was Elite's purpose. They provided the services no one else could or would.

Elite Connections was a matchmaking service, a concierge for whatever you needed. I had heard a little about them in the past, but they had seemed more like an urban legend than anything. I hadn't personally known anyone to actually have used their services and didn't have any need for them, so I had no reason to seek them out or to even believe they existed, or that they could deliver on what they promised.

Until now.

This morning, I still hadn't believed it. Even as I readied my home for a guest, I hadn't really believed anyone would be coming. I had been wracking my brain for old friends I could call in favors with, but I didn't know how I was going to sell any sort of relationship, and I very much doubted my ability to meet someone new in a timely enough manner to satisfy Lexi's plan.

I needed a miracle, and while I believed in Lexi, I didn't believe Elite would really come through.

Now, I knew Elite weren't miracle workers, since they had delivered my personal hell.

They had dragged up her, a ghost from my past who I couldn't stand, who couldn't stand me, and yet I was somehow supposed to sell the world on us being in love. Even the best actress would struggle with that, and I wasn't the best. There was a reason acting never worked out for me.

"It won't work," I told Lexi. "There has to be another way. There's no way we could sell this."

"Speak for yourself. Some of us with talent are up to any role."

Maya couldn't be implying she actually wanted to go through with this. "You can't mean that. You think you could pull off being in love with me?"

She dry heaved dramatically. I rolled my eyes at her. "No one said anything about being in love. Your girlfriend, yes. Being in love is off the table."

"The press won't buy anything unbelievable," I warned her.

She smirked. "Trust me, I'll be believable enough that when I humiliate and dump your ass, everyone will buy it."

I shook my head, turning back to Lexi. "There's no way. We'll have to work something else out."

"If you're finally admitting you can't act to save your life, then I'll gladly take a fat check from you and be on my way, but I was promised money and I'm not leaving until I get it."

Maya hadn't changed a bit.

I crossed my arms. "This has nothing to do with my acting skills and everything to do with not believing for a second that you could sell this," I bluffed.

She looked at me in disgust. "What? Little miss perfect needs me to audition for her? Fine. Although I don't know why I'm bothering, since no one else would put up with your ass long enough to do the job."

She looked at Lexi. "You're the judge. You decide if I'm good enough."

As I watched, she took a deep breath and her face changed, her hard gaze turning molten as she raked her eyes over my body. I tried and failed to suppress a shiver. *Get it together, Savannah. This is Maya for god's sake.* Clearly, I had let my dry spell go on for too long if even Maya could get this reaction out of me. I leveled a "is that the best you've got" look at her as she started to cross the room. She didn't just walk over to me, she sauntered.

She backed me into the wall behind me, pressing her body to mine, pushing me against the wall harder than necessary. The breath left my body. She ran her fingers through my hair and I leaned into her touch. She licked her lips and I couldn't stop my eyes following the movement of her tongue.

"Baby, you're looking a little flushed. It's a little hot in here. Why don't I help you get a little more comfortable?"

Before I could understand her meaning or respond, she spun me around into the wall, my back pressing up against her. She slowly brushed her fingers through my hair, pushing it to one side.

I felt her breath on my now exposed neck and she leaned in and whispered, "Seen enough yet, Hollywood?"

I gasped as she licked my neck and then started peppering it with kisses. At the same time, her hands were pulling off my blazer. As she slid it down my shoulders, she nipped my neck and I gasped.

She threw the blazer behind her and turned me back around, leaning her arm against the wall over me. I gulped. She leaned in.

"Okay cut," Lexi said. "I get it, you guys have chemistry, but for this to work, you guys will have to be able to get along, too. Less seduction, more affection."

I was still trying to catch my breath, but Maya just rolled her shoulders back and said, "Fine, give me a second."

She moved away, crossing back to the other side of the room, and I was happy to have a moment to collect myself. She was making my head spin.

She turned around, and again was transformed. Her posture became more relaxed and her hard gaze turned soft, and familiar. I sucked in a breath at the warmth in her deep brown eyes. I hadn't seen them look at me like that in so long, like she missed me, like she cared. The last time I had seen her, her eyes had burned with betrayal and hatred, and seeing her soften like this cracked some of my resolve.

As I watched, she ran her fingers through her hair, looking at the ground. She glanced up quickly and met my eye and broke into a goofy grin. I couldn't help smiling back. She crossed the room to me, picking up the discarded blazer as she did. When she reached me, she pulled me into her arms, holding me tight for a moment before letting me go and gingerly lacing her fingers through mine.

She looked concerned for a moment. "You seem a little cold, love. Here, take my jacket."

She slid my blazer back on and tucked a stray piece of hair behind my ear. She leaned in painfully slowly. I waited for Lexi to interrupt. Any second now she would call cut. Any moment ... but then Maya's lips were on mine. Sweet, but sure. Soft, but knowing. I couldn't have told you my name.

"You're hired!" I heard a voice say.

Maya pulled away with a smirk. "Obviously. You're desperate and I'm damn good."

She was. Too good, and I was in trouble.

"Well," she said, looking at Lexi, "now that that's settled, why don't you show me to my room."

CHAPTER 8

I glared at Lexi as Maya swore.

"You can't be serious," I told her.

She had brought us both to my room, where all of Maya's things had been brought. They were supposed to be in one of the many guest rooms, but here they were, and when I tried to move them, Lexi had stepped in front of the door.

She looked apologetic, but didn't budge. "You can take it up with Clarice when she gets here. I'm just following instructions.

I just blinked at her. "You work for me."

She chuckled. "Yes, and until your contract with Elite ends, I also answer to them. You didn't like my plan. This was the route you decided to take. We agreed to their terms, so unless they say otherwise, I'm very much serious. You two are going to eat, sleep, and breathe as a real couple until you break up. Elite says it's the only way, and, apparently, they don't half ass anything."

I looked at Maya. "There's no way you're staying in here with me."

"Like I want to."

"They didn't even move a second bed in here. It's not like anyone would know. They can't be serious. It's not like the paparazzi's going to follow us into the bedroom."

"You'd be surprised what they can see," a voice said.

I turned around and was surprised to see a short woman with a strict black bob and thick glasses making herself right at home in my oversized pink lounge chair in the corner of the room.

"You can't be serious," Maya asked.

I knew from experience, she wasn't exaggerating much. The press had eyes everywhere.

She chuckled and opened her purse, riffling through. "Okay, so maybe the paparazzi won't see, but Clarice will," she said, pulling out a device, that it took me a moment to recognize as a baby monitor, and setting it up on the bureau facing the bed.

"Who the fuck is Clarice and why is she watching me sleep?" Maya asked.

I wouldn't have used those words, but I couldn't help but agree.

The woman laughed. "Silly me, I'm Clarice. I'm your relationship and acting coach."

I was shocked by that. Elite was really rubbing salt in the wound. I knew I wasn't a good actress, but I didn't think an acting coach was what we needed.

Maya crossed her arms. "Like I need an acting coach. I eat, sleep, and breath acting."

Clarice just waved her hand dismissively. "Yeah, yeah, I've heard it all before. You don't need an acting coach, you're professionals. Yada yada. I get it, but that's on set. This is role immersion like you've never experienced. In order to sell it, we have to make it believable. If you two are sleeping in separate rooms, the world might not know, but they would be able to tell. The chemistry would be all wrong. But Clarice doesn't fail and doesn't do surprises, so this is staying here to make sure you take me seriously."

"I really think she's serious," Maya said, turning to me. "They're your dogs. Call them off."

"I didn't hire Clarice! I don't even know Clarice!"

"Very true. I'm on Elite's payroll, and you would be wise to be kinder to me if you plan to continue to stay on it, too," Clarice said matter-of-factly to Maya. I waited with bated breath for whatever pointed remark Maya was going to make to her, but she surprised me by staying quiet. Maybe she reserved her malice for me, or maybe she needed this job worse than I thought. She wasn't even looking at Clarice anymore; she was glaring at me instead.

Clarice looked at me. "It was all in Elite's contract you signed. Your manager assured me you had read it fully."

I had meant to, I really had, but I knew either way I was going to sign it. It wasn't like I had any other choice. I had fallen asleep somewhere around page 6 and never actually made it to the end. When my alarm went off the next morning, I had hastily signed it and returned it to Lexi.

Clearly, that was a bigger mistake than I had thought.

"Your manager assured me you would prefer the monitors instead of me staying here with you both."

"Monitors? Plural?" Maya asked.

"Staying here with us?" I asked. I started to panic, feeling my small slice of freedom slipping through my grasp.

"I won't have to. The monitors will do the trick. You'll know I'm watching. Day in and day out, I'll be watching, so put on a good show," she said, winking at me. I blushed a deep red, and she laughed.

I glanced over at Maya, who was still staring at Clarice like she had five heads. Good to know I wasn't the only one stupid enough to not have fully read the contract.

"Elite also sent along your new stylist, the elegant, extraordinary Miss Lucy Fur."

As if out of thin air, right on cue, in came a gorgeous black Drag Queen in what had to be eight-inch heels with a bright red flowing cape with flames embroidered down the length of it. "Darhling, I'm much more than a stylist. Say hello to your Fairy DragMother, stylist, fashionista extraordinaire. And please call me Miss Lucy." She looked at Maya and said, "Honey, I'm going to take you from zero to hero."

She glared at them, but Miss Lucy had already turned to me. "And you, darhling, you're already an icon, but I'm here to bring you from icon to bi-con. We're gonna bust those closet doors wide open and scream 'Hello world! I'm here, I'm queer, and you better get used to it.'"

I gulped. I knew I only had a few weeks left before the world knew, before I told everyone, but this was making it feel more real.

I smiled as much as I could. Clarice and Miss Lucy were here to help me, and as crappy as the situation was, it wasn't their fault. It wouldn't kill me to be kind to them.

"Thank you both so much. I appreciate what you're doing for me more than you know. I'll try my best to follow your lead."

"That's all we ask," Clarice said, grinning.

Maya's jaw dropped open. "What?!" she exclaimed.

"What?" I asked, looking at her, confused.

"You can't actually mean you're going to go along with this?"

I shrugged. "I mean, yeah. I don't have much of a choice, and I'm grateful they're here to help."

She scowled at me. "Likely story. What about me, Hollywood? You grateful I'm here, too?"

I couldn't hide my grimace. "Grateful's a bit strong."

"At least we agree on something."

Clarice looked at Miss Lucy. "We have our work cut out for us."

The rest of the day flew by and I was pleasantly surprised to have to spend shockingly little alone time with Maya. Clarice and Miss Lucy kept us busy going over what was expected of us.

We only had a few weeks until my coming out, and then three more weeks until my album launch, and things needed to be perfect. I wouldn't let my soon to be ex-husband and his crazy rumors ruin this. I had to keep reminding myself that was why I was doing this, so my work could stand on its own, so Connor didn't get dragged into this mess. *Connor! Fuck. I was going to have to fool Connor and the rest of the band, too.* I was embarrassed it hadn't occurred to me before now just how far I was going to have to take this. They were like family to me and it was going to be really weird keeping this from them, but the less people that knew the better. I was just worried I might not be able to convince the band Maya and I were together.

I was screwed. I didn't know how I was going to get through this, but I was counting on my team and on Elite to make it happen.

From the amount I knew Lexi was paying them from my accounts, it was a fair expectation for things to run smoothly.

Why anyone in their right mind thought pairing me with Maya was a good idea, though, was beyond me. Maybe they thought it would be better to bring on someone who already knew me, or thought they did, but they had to have known things didn't end well between us. They had to have known we hadn't spoken since Hollywood High stopped filming, and that I was more or less the reason it did. Unofficially, of course.

Officially, the show stopped filming because it had reached its peak and we all had other commitments, but in reality, the show wasn't allowed to continue. It wasn't in the network's best interest to keep the show going. We all knew that. The network's executives had bigger plans for me, and my contract allowed them to do what they wanted with me. To them, the show was at a natural ending point. Everyone else in the crew had seen the writing on the wall, so why it hit Maya so hard was beyond me.

I didn't understand, nor did I care to try after how she had treated me and was still treating me. I didn't care to be in a room with her ever again, and as my manager, Lexi, of all people, should have known that and made sure it didn't happen.

I would have to have a serious talk with her. This wasn't just a blindside, but a serious concern. If Maya and I couldn't pull this off, I stood to lose everything. With my failed marriage, it felt like my career was the only thing I had going for me right now, and I couldn't lose that. I couldn't let him take that from me, too. Not when he was trying to take everything else from me.

I had no choice. This had to work.

It seemed like Maya was fully committed, who knows why, but it seemed I could at least count myself lucky that she wouldn't be trying to humiliate me.

Until our public breakup, at least.

She had made that much clear, and I was already thinking I was going to regret not asking more questions and not getting more control over the process with Elite, but only time would tell.

THE BI-CON PROJECT
THE TIMELINE

Week 1: (5/18)

Training – trust exercises, getting to know each other
games, communication training

Week 2: (5/25)

Continued training
A test run in a semi-public place to see how they are
in public together

Week 3: (6/1)

Savannah and Maya get caught getting hot and heavy
in public by the paparazzi
Savannah comes out on socials just in time for Pride
Month
Maybe photo ops at a Pride Festival depending on
how her coming out goes

Weeks 4 and 5: (6/8 and 6/15)
Rehearsals for the album launch performance
Savannah and Maya are out on a lot of public dates

Week 6: (6/22)
Album launch performance, Maya performs with Savannah on stage

Week 7: (6/29)
The wrap up, they have a couple more public events, but are seen less together
Maybe Savannah or Maya is spotted out with someone else, just a friend but it would get people speculating

Week 8: (7/6)
The breakup, Maya publicly breaks up with Savannah in a place of Savannah's choosing and the contract ends

CHAPTER 9

SAVANNAH

When Clarice and Miss Lucy finally left for the night after going over the schedule for our next two months with us extensively, I was exhausted and couldn't wait to curl up in my bed. I didn't know where Maya had ended up and was too tired to care. I opened the door to my room, not even bothering to turn the light on or change. I was too tired. I just shuffled over to the bed and flopped down.

I jolted up when the bed was harder than I expected and let out a yelled, "Hey!"

Maya.

"What are you doing here?" I said, groaning.

I could hear the annoyance in her voice. "It's not like I had a choice." It was too dark to see anything more than her shape, but I could have sworn I heard her eyes roll.

"Well, move over. You're on my side," I said, shoving into her, trying to push her to the other side.

"Not happening. The world might treat you like royalty, but I'm definitely not doing your bidding. If we're making it through the next couple months together, it's better you learn that now."

I sighed, hating that she was right. Not about claiming my side of the bed, but about the fact that I was going to have to play nice if this was going to work.

"Fine, but I'm turning the light on first. I can't see shit in here."

She didn't say anything, but I heard rustling. When I made it to the switch and flicked on the lights, she groaned. It took a moment for my eyes to adjust enough to see her. She had certainly made herself at home and was using my favorite silk blanket. It was perfect for the warm nights we'd been having.

I couldn't help but laugh, seeing that the remaining blankets and pillows had all been piled in the middle of the bed. A regular Mount Everest of comfort dividing the bed, but not evenly. She had barely left me room to lie down.

This was going to be a long couple of months.

I made my way to the bed and sat down, shoving the blanket and pillow wall a little toward her side.

"Hey! Watch it!" she yelled.

"It's not my fault you're taking up the whole bed," I ground out, losing my patience faster and faster by the second.

"And it's not my fault we're in this situation. I'll touch you in public for money, but don't expect me to do it in private for free."

My mouth dropped open as the significance of the pillow and blanket wall hit me. She might not be comfortable with this. I blanched at the thought, but when

I saw her shooting me a look of disgust, anger boiled up in me.

She agreed to do this. Sure, she hadn't known it was going to be me, but she signed up for this. She stayed even after finding out it was me. I wouldn't let myself have any sympathy for her, especially since I apparently disgusted her.

She had no right to treat me like she was and if this was how she was going to be for the next couple months, I didn't know if I could handle it, and more importantly, there was no way anyone would believe for a second that we were in love.

"We're screwed," I said quietly, rolled over, grabbed the remote for the lights, and turned them off.

"You can say that again," she said quietly.

At least we could agree on something.

CHAPTER 10

SAVANNAH

I blinked down at the question cards in my hand before looking up at Clarice. She couldn't be serious.

"What does this have to do with anything?" I asked, trying not to snap at her. I kept having to remind myself that this wasn't her fault, and that she was just doing her job.

The card I was blinking down at read, "Favorite Color."

From the glare Maya was sending Clarice's way, I guessed hers wasn't any more relevant seeming.

"If you want people to believe you two care about each other, you have to start by caring about each other."

I grimaced, and Maya groaned.

"At least you two agree on something," Clarice said. "But to get the public to believe you care about each other, you have to care enough to get to know the small details."

"Like what flavor toothpaste we use?" Maya said skeptically.

I laughed. I couldn't help it.

"I got 'Favorite Color.'"

She rolled her eyes and turned back to Clarice. "How is this possibly going to help?"

"You ladies just have to trust the process. The quicker you answer, the quicker we can move on."

"Fine. Purple and green."

I just blinked at her, surprised. Clarice shook her head. "You have to pick one."

She stared back at her. "I did. Mine's green, hers is purple."

She was right, of course, but it surprised me she remembered, especially when most of the world assumed pink was my favorite. I did like pink, but I had to wear far too much of it on Hollywood High and for my concerts afterward to have had it remain my favorite. I used to complain to her all the time about the Barbie amount of pink they had me in. It warmed my heart just a little that she remembered.

Clarice glanced at me and took my surprised face for confirmation. She clapped her hands together. "Now we're getting somewhere. Maybe there's hope for you two after all. Now, toothpaste flavors, go!"

"Mint," I said while Maya said, "Bubblegum," at the same time.

I gaped at her. "Bubblegum? What are you, a child?"

She scowls. "Mint? How boring and basic. I shouldn't be surprised."

"Nor should I," Clarice added. I looked at her in shock before she clarified, "I shouldn't be surprised that we've taken one step forward and two steps back.

No worries. I'll have you two comfortable in no time. Next card."

The rest of the afternoon passed by like that. It turned out Clarice had started us out on the easy cards and that things got more and more personal with each card. I found myself surprised at how much I was opening up and how much Maya was, too.

I learned more of her favorites, getting to know the woman she'd grown into, who I was surprised to find wasn't as different from the girl I had known as I had thought.

We even caught ourselves laughing together when we shared embarrassing moments. I had tried to swallow my laughter when she finished telling her story, but I hadn't been able to. She had thrown a pillow at me and I burst into more laughter, equal parts relieved and surprised when she followed suit.

A few more cards later, Clarice's phone rang, and it was like the spell had been broken.

Clarice excused herself, cuing us to continue, but without her here, with just me and Maya sitting together, it hit me who I was opening up to. It really hit me how bad of an idea this was and how much deeper things were getting than I planned or was comfortable with.

One look at her, seeing she was already glowering at me, told me she felt the same.

It wasn't until she stalked off after throwing her cards on the floor that I realized why. Her card said,

"When was the last time you felt betrayed by someone you cared about?"

It was probably for the best. Neither of our answers to that question would have helped inspire connection.

CHAPTER 11

MAYA

Trust exercises, what a joke. As if there were any sort of exercises, trust or otherwise, that would get me to trust her after the stunt she pulled.

Yes, it was years ago, but it still felt like yesterday, and if I was being honest, the passing time only made me more bitter about it. Seeing how far her career had grown while mine shriveled up continued to eat away at me. Especially with my family struggling for money while she had more than any one person could ever need.

After the betrayal question, I had refused to keep going with the cards, but now I was wishing I had. Clarice was a little too excited about the trust falls. She directed me to stand in front of Hollywood and fall back; I flat out refused. Yes, she hadn't done anything outright cruel yet, but I knew her. She was just bidding her time. She was going to let me fall on my ass. I knew she would.

Clarice groaned. "Fine. I'll demonstrate. Savannah, why don't you stand in front of me, close your eyes, and when you're ready, fall backward. I'll be right here to catch you."

Hollywood moved into position and her eyes fluttered closed. She crossed her arms over her chest, took a deep breath, and fell back. Unsurprisingly, but disappointingly, Clarice caught her. Then she righted her and Hollywood opened her eyes.

"See?" Clarice said to us both of us. "That wasn't so hard, was it? Now why don't you girls give it a try."

"Fine, but I'm not going first," I scoffed.

Hollywood glared at me. "I literally just went."

"So, you're nice and warmed up," I said, moving behind her.

I couldn't help letting my eyes trail to her ass, couldn't help leaning a little closer and saying, "Besides, the view is much better from back here."

I was as surprised by my words as she was. She heated and seemed to be trying to decide if that was an insult or compliment. It was a little of both.

She crossed her arms again and hesitated. "Come on, Hollywood, we don't have all day," I said, goading her.

A moment later, she fell back into me. I was tempted for half a second to step aside, but I stayed put. I might not care about her, but I cared about this job, about the things it would do for me and my career. I didn't care about her, and seeing her fall on her tight little ass would've been hilarious, but not worth throwing away this opportunity.

As much as I hated how she had gained her fame on the broken backs of myself and everyone else involved with Hollywood High, I would be a fool not to use her now that the opportunity presented itself.

Plus, Hollywood and me as a couple would be a big deal to the fans of the show. Some of the show's fans used to joke about our chemistry. There had even been some unhinged, concerning fanfiction about it. Concerning since we were only seventeen at that point and playing high schoolers. But the second news spread that Savannah Hollywood, *the* Savannah Hollywood, Hollywood's It girl, was bisexual and dating her old washed-up costar, I would be all the rage again.

People would flock to stream the old seasons of our show looking for clues, over-analyzing the non-existent chemistry we had had, and all of a sudden, I would be a household name.

Yes, it would be next to hers, but I could handle that. It would skyrocket me to fame overnight. I would be making the tabloids again, and not just on the "Where are they now" lists.

I would go from washed up to a hot commodity, all for dealing with Hollywood for a couple months.

It was only two months, and then I got to humiliate her ass and dump her publicly. We could go our separate ways again. Except new opportunities would be knocking at my door then.

So, I caught her.

I felt her exhale her relief as she let herself relax into me, the tension easing from her body. Apparently, she was just as unsure that I was going to catch her as I had been. I couldn't understand for the life of me why she had let herself fall at all when she expected to be let down.

It almost made me feel sympathy for her. Almost. But that was the difference between us. If someone let me down, I wasn't turning my back to them or trusting them again for anything.

I told Clarice as much until she finally gave up on that particular exercise. She put us through various other exercises that she said were supposed to improve our communication and instill trust, but despite me following her commands, I knew it wouldn't work. The girl across from me had proved long ago that I couldn't trust her. No amount of money in the world could make me make that same mistake again.

THE BI-CON PROJECT
WEEK ONE UPDATE

Getting these two to work together and get to know each other again is proving more difficult than expected. I hadn't thought it would be easy by any means, but I hoped they would have some sense of the importance of working together. It seems the only thing they have in common is their distrust of one another. Savannah is trying hard, but to be fair, she arguably has more to lose in all of this.

It's clear Maya is trying as well, but even clearer that she is struggling to let go of the past enough to move forward and work together with Savannah. She still sees Savannah as her opponent. At least their arguments haven't spiraled out of control. They dealt with my lessons in arguing about as well as the other lessons, but I'm hoping that it will prove helpful when they actually argue.

They have been sniping at each other, but haven't had a real argument. Right now, Savannah seems to be taking whatever Maya is dishing out. She hasn't rose to Maya's challenges and flown off the handle yet, but I feel like it's just a matter of time before Maya pushes her too far.

Maya is clearly still hurt and Savannah is struggling to navigate her and Maya's feelings while still working toward her own goals. I have faith that I can force them onto common ground, but it won't be easy, and they're nowhere near ready for a public appearance yet.

I was hoping sharing a room would force them to bond a little more, but that doesn't seem to be the case yet. The baby monitors I don't actually monitor have been enough so far to keep them sharing a room, which is promising at least. I need to push them further and harder to have them ready in time, though. Hopefully if I'm able to continue to make myself their common enemy, they'll see each other as allies.

More updates to follow

Clarice

CHAPTER 12

SAVANNAH

After a week and a half of Clarice's nonstop rigorous tests and games, we were finally being let out of the house, and I was thrilled. Yes, it was with Maya and it was a test, but at least we were getting out of the house. I would take what I could get.

Six more weeks, I kept reminding myself. Only six more weeks and then I wouldn't have to see her again. I could do this. Maybe after I could even find myself a real girlfriend.

I hadn't had much time for dating anyone lately with work taking up most of my time, but it would be nice to have someone to come home to.

Someone who wasn't *Maya*, I thought. Someone I actually wanted to be around, who actually liked me.

I looked out the window of the town car, trying my best to ignore the eyes I could feel on me.

She was glaring at me; I knew she was. I didn't have to look to know I was right. She hadn't stopped glaring at me since Miss Lucy had given us these outfits.

I had thought they were going to lean into a feminine look for me. I was right. They had put me in a bright pink dress that hugged my chest before flaring out in a skirt that ended just above my knees. With my blonde hair curled at the ends, I looked like a Barbie, just like I had on Hollywood High.

Maya's outfit, on the other hand, was so much more feminine than she seemed comfortable with. She was wearing a lacey white bustier top and a floor length grey maxi skirt with slits on both sides. If it hadn't been for her signature leather jacket, she wouldn't have been recognizable. She was still glaring at me, but I couldn't bring myself to feel much sympathy. Especially since the clothes were paid for by me.

I heard Clarice talking and realized I had zoned out. I listened for a moment, long enough to tell she wasn't talking to me, before looking back out the window.

I had wanted to take the limo and couldn't for the life of me understand why we didn't. I thought the whole point of today, and of our dating in general, was to draw attention to ourselves. Not that I really cared how we got there, just that in the limo I would've been able to sit a lot further from Maya, which would've made our night on the town a lot more enjoyable.

The town car was fine, but we were sitting right next to each other. Her arm was resting on the middle seat, her hand almost touching my seat belt it was so far past the middle, and I could still feel her glaring at me, daring me to protest.

I didn't. I couldn't care less, but if she needed to indulge in her weird display of dominance, then I would let her, for now. It didn't matter. The only thing that mattered was that she didn't screw this up for me. I had so much riding on this and she was the last person in the world I would normally trust to help me out.

I was thankful that she at least seemed to be taking this as seriously as I was. I just hoped she was still as good an actress as I remembered and could handle this.

I had told Lexi several times that I didn't believe Maya would keep this a secret. I still wasn't sure she would, but Lexi assured me that Elite didn't mess around with their NDAs and that Maya wouldn't breathe a word. If she did, they would sue her for all that she was worth, which, based on what I guessed from our present predicament, wasn't much.

At least, I assumed if she wasn't in need of money, her ass would've been out the door the second she saw it was me. I wondered, not for the first time since then, what it was that kept her here. I hoped she wasn't struggling. I didn't have to like her to not want her to suffer. No one deserved to be in a bad enough financial situation that they couldn't afford to turn down a job like this.

I had thought about helping her out more, giving her more than was required by our contract, but I knew she wouldn't take anything from me. Even back when we were kids, she was quick to refuse anything she saw as charity.

Besides, I thought selfishly, her having a big financial stake in this too made it a little easier to trust her. I knew I couldn't actually trust her, but I hoped I could trust her to act in her own best interest and go along with Elite's plan.

I did still have some concerns though, concerns that I shared with Lexi. I probably shouldn't have. She never let anything go and the moment I expressed my continued concern, she did some digging into Maya's life. She hired a private investigator. She didn't tell me what she found, but she assured me this morning that it was enough to make sure Maya stayed quiet, and enough to discredit her if she didn't. I didn't ask what it was Lexi found. It felt sleazy that she had done it and I didn't want to know. I understood why she felt like she had to in order to protect me, but I didn't love that she did it without my permission or approval. I wouldn't have approved. At least, I wanted to believe I wouldn't have.

I knew how big the stakes were, how much was riding on this, but that didn't change the fact that I didn't like the idea of blackmail. Too many times I'd had paparazzi, "friends", and even fans try to blackmail me and while they usually didn't go through with their threats, it didn't stop me from feeling violated. I hated the way it made me feel, and even though I couldn't stand Maya, I would never do that to anyone, not even my worst enemy.

I had made that clear to Lexi, and she assured me she wouldn't use it, but I couldn't help noticing she never said she got rid of the evidence.

The song playing in the car changed and the familiar tune instantly pulled me out of my thoughts, grabbing my attention. It was my first ever single, the one I released right after Hollywood High ended. The one that launched me to predetermined stardom.

"Change it," Maya ground out. I turned, surprised by the sudden noise, and saw she was glaring at me.

"You know I don't control the radio, right?" I asked, rolling my eyes.

"Yes, but you do control the station. Change it or have your driver pull over. I'm not going any further listening to that crap."

I did have a remote in the back, but I hadn't touched it since we had gotten into the car. I didn't even know where it was.

"Fine, fine. Hold on a second, let me find it."

She moved closer to me, halfway over the middle seat now, and said, "I know what you're doing and it won't work. You're not going to get me to quit."

I stopped looking for the remote and turned back to her. "I'm not doing anything except trying to cater to your crazy demands. I'm sorry you don't like the music, but I don't have a damn clue where the remote is, and we're almost there, so either you can shut up and deal with it, or you can walk."

"Pull over," she said to the driver.

I felt the car speed up.

Maya went for the door handle, pulled it and pushed on the door, but it didn't open.

She tried again while I watched and again had no luck. She swore loudly, before turning to me, and saying, "What the fuck, Hollywood?"

I glared back at her and was about to tell her off when Clarice cleared her throat in the front seat and turned around to face us, the disappointment in her eyes magnified to an almost comical degree by her large glasses.

"Actually, that was me," she said. "Child locks, and a good thing, too, since apparently you two are choosing to act like children."

Maya turned her glare to Clarice, and I piped up, "That's not fair! I didn't even do anything!"

Clarice crossed her arms while looking at us. "Maybe not, but listening to your complaining, you sound like a child."

I crossed my arms and then uncrossed them a moment later when I realized that my pouting was just further proving her point.

Clarice looked at Maya and held up the missing remote. "And the music was me, too. A stress test that I can easily see you failed. Clearly, I have more work cut out for me than I thought. Elite will be hearing from me about a raise, because you two are no picnic."

Neither of us said anything. I was too embarrassed. Even Maya seemed too chastised to say anything else.

"If you two can't call a truce for one evening for long enough to have dinner, then we're calling this off right now. The world will continue to believe your ex-husband's rumors," she said to me before turning to Maya and saying, "And I'll call Elite and let them know not to cut you your check."

I started to panic. She couldn't do that, could she? Could she really just stop helping us? Before I could ask, Maya beat me to it, "But you can't do that!"

Clarice's face hardened, making her look, if possible, even more stern. "I can and I will. If you two can't convince me this is going to work, then I'm sure as hell not putting my neck on the line for either of you. Elite trusts me. I've never failed them before and I won't now. So, either you two start acting like adults or I turn the car around. Understood?"

"Fine," Maya said, but I heard her mumble under her breath, "She's not even driving. How's she gonna turn us around?"

I couldn't stop the giggle from leaving my lips and immediately put my hand in front of my mouth. Clarice's eyes whipped to me. "Savannah, did you have something to say?"

"No, ma'am. I can handle this."

She nodded, turning back around in her seat. I wasn't sure if she meant for me to hear or not, but under her breath she added, "You better be right."

I hoped I was.

CHAPTER 13

MAYA

When we pulled up, I tried to seem as unimpressed as possible, but I'm sure the mask slipped. I was excited, of course I was. This was Rizzo's, legendary when it came to Italian. It catered to the stars. You had to be somebody to get a reservation, and even then, they normally had a wait a few months long.

I wondered if Elite had pulled the strings or if Hollywood's popularity did. I hoped it was Elite. I couldn't count the amount of times I had tried to get a reservation here. They never told me outright that I wasn't good enough, but they never called me back, either.

I looked around and was surprised there were only a few paparazzi out front. It didn't seem possible. Normally, the place was crawling with them.

I looked over at Hollywood to see if she knew any more than I did, but she looked just as surprised. Good. At least I wasn't the only one in the dark.

I turned to look at Clarice and saw she was smiling. She must be responsible then. I wondered what sort of miracle she had to pull to get us a quiet night here, because that was certainly no small feat.

I smirked to myself, thinking that I hoped it cost Hollywood a fortune.

When the car stopped, I went for the door, but it still didn't open. A quick glance over at Hollywood showed she had the same result.

"Aw come on. We're here now," I said to Clarice.

"And you'll wait until I'm ready to open the doors," she said, nodding to the driver who put the car in park. Clarice looked at Hollywood quickly and then at me for longer. "I expect an Oscar winning performance out there."

I rolled my eyes. It would be. I would have to be nothing short of flawless to convince anyone I was okay with being within fifty feet of Hollywood, but I was a goddamn actress and I could do this. There was too much riding on this for me to fail, so I would make it work.

"Understood?" she asked, looking between us.

I looked at Hollywood, quirking my eyebrow at her. "What do you think, Hollywood? You up for the challenge?"

She watched me for a moment, before nodding.

Clarice looked between us and after a moment something in our faces must have satisfied her because she said, "Okay, so Lawrence is going to get out and open Maya's door. Then you're expected to walk around the car and open Savannah's door."

I grimaced. "So, I'm waiting on her?"

Hollywood groaned. "No; you're being chivalrous."

Clarice smiled. "Exactly. It doesn't matter if you were royalty, she's your girlfriend and you're trying to woo her. You'll open her door."

"Woo? What is this, the 19th century?"

Hollywood laughed, and I glared at her.

This so wasn't funny. Of course, little miss perfect was okay with me waiting on her hand and foot.

"In order for this to be believable, you've got to be seen trying to impress her, and you both have to be on your best behavior."

"Why can't she be trying to impress me?" I asked, still annoyed.

Clarice shook her head. "That doesn't fit the narrative we're pushing. You've been out for a while now, she hasn't. If this were real, she'd be a little more nervous and timid. It would be your job to help her feel comfortable, to help her come out of her shell, so that's what we're doing."

As much as it still annoyed me, I knew she was right.

"Are we clear on the plan?" Clarice said, daring us to argue with her.

We both nodded. The sooner we got out of the car, the sooner I could indulge in as much gourmet cuisine as Hollywood's wallet could buy, which was sure to be a lot.

At Clarice's signal, the driver hopped out of the car and came back to my door, opening it for me.

I jumped out, eager to get this over with, but one look at the driver had me remembering my role here.

I took a deep breath and slowed my steps. I wanted to be self-assured, but not arrogant, falling hard but not a fool in love. I wanted the world to know I was serious about her and our relationship and putting my all into it without looking like she was the one in charge. I had to make this seem like a whirlwind romance that she was swept up in. I wanted to leave enough of a mark on her that she would have to publicly mourn our breakup. I wanted the public to think our love was so epic that no other woman could ever measure up to me in her eyes.

It was a hell of a task, but I could take it one day at a time, and tonight, I just had to make it believable that I liked her. Believable that we were friends going out for dinner, believable that maybe it could be something more. Tonight was a test; low pressure because the speculation wouldn't really start until she came out to the world. Then everything we did would be under a microscope. Tonight was going to feel easy in comparison.

Tonight, we could just be two friends out on the town. Me and Hollywood being seen together was sure to be enough to cause questions and attention. I hadn't been quiet about the fact that we weren't friends, so even selling that was going to be hard. I groaned, thinking about how much more difficult I had made this for myself by being as outspoken as I was about my feelings toward her.

I took one more breath and rounded to the other side of the car, shedding my own feelings and stepping into my role. I was cautious, but hopeful. Confident, but knew this was important. I wanted to make Savannah like me, wanted to make Savannah fall hard for me, and I'd be damned if this proved to be the one role I couldn't master.

I let the hope fill my eyes, and a lightness come through my step. I strode to her door with purpose, listening for the sounds of cameras clicking, for the bright lights of their flashes, and was mildly annoyed when they didn't come.

But of course, they didn't. I was just me, some washed up has been. I felt the anger surfacing at the so-called star in the car who had pushed me out of the spotlight. I took a quick breath. No, tonight I wasn't Maya Ryder, washed up actress. Tonight, I was reuniting with a long-lost friend and rekindling a budding romance. Tonight was the start of something beautiful. To the rest of the world, it was going to be the start of a beautiful romance. To me, it was the restarting of a beautiful, hopefully long, career. Tonight was the start of my comeback, and nothing could be more beautiful than that.

I gripped the handle and pulled open the door. Without giving it a second thought, I offered her my hand, helping her out of the car like the perfect girlfriend I was. I felt her fingers grip mine. She was surprisingly strong. Using my arm for support, she descended from the car. The moment her heels hit the ground, I heard the camera clicks and saw the flashes. I narrowly avoided rolling my eyes.

Of course, the second she stepped out, they would pay attention, but they were paying attention to us both now and that was what mattered. It was show-time.

I watched her right herself and move her hand from my arm to smooth out the non-existent wrin-kles on her dress, and couldn't take my eyes away from her. There was no denying she was beautiful. Her soft blonde hair fell in waves around her and her bright pink dress that paid homage to her time on Hollywood High should have looked childish on her, but even that dress couldn't hide her curves. Even in that dress, she was every bit the sex symbol she had become, and I couldn't help but feel envious. I held my arm out for her again and she laced her fingers through my arm, holding onto me.

It was only fifty feet to the restaurant door, but I was glad we had Hollywood's bodyguard who doubled as her driver with us when the few paparazzi ran over to us. They pushed into each other, calling her name. I heard one of them ask, "Who's that with her?"

Another yelled out, "Hollywood, who's your friend?"

I wanted to groan, but I held it in. Of course, they knew Hollywood well enough, but didn't even recog-nize me from the same show. Her guard and Clarice sandwiched us between them and a moment later, a couple of staff from the restaurant came running out over to us.

To Hollywood, they said, "I'm so sorry, Miss Hollywood. Had we known you were coming, we would have been sure to clear the place of these vultures. Shoo! Go on, get out of the ladies' way!" he said louder, and the paparazzi listened and actually moved aside. I blinked in surprise at that before remembering myself and ushering my date toward the restaurant. The man led us to the hostess stand and then asked Hollywood, "Your usual table for you and your friend?" he added after a brief glance at me.

I fought to keep the disbelief and anger off my face. I had tried so many times to get a reservation here, and Hollywood had a regular table. Of course she did.

Clarice butted in, "No, actually something more private, if that can be arranged. They have some business to discuss that shouldn't be overheard, if you know what I mean."

I didn't even know what she meant, but he nodded quickly. "That can be arranged. Just one moment." He almost ran out back, and Clarice turned to us. "That'll buy you girls some space and time to work on making this believable. I expect nothing bad to make headlines, understood?"

I glanced at Hollywood, who nodded and I quickly agreed, too. If it was going to be so easy for her with her "superior" acting skills, I would make sure to show her I could do this in my sleep.

The man came back looking relieved and said, "A private room for the ladies, just this way." He gestured for us to follow him.

I went to move, but Hollywood stayed put. Clarice hadn't moved yet either. She grinned at the both of us and said, "We'll be outside when you're done. Have a good time, girls."

I watched Hollywood's face go from confusion to panic to resignation in a split second. Apparently, she hadn't realized she'd be alone with me. It looked like it was making her nervous. I smirked before giving into my impulse and pulling her in to me. With my arm wrapped around her waist, I ushered her in the direction the man had gone. Quietly, so no one could overhear, I whispered into her ear, "What's the matter, Hollywood? Worried? I promise I'll go easy on you."

Seeing the shade of red her face turned made me wish the paparazzi had been allowed in because that would've made for a great photo slapped on the front page of a tabloid. What a shame.

I felt her pull a little away from me and held her in place. If I was playing this role, you better believe I was going to play it well.

The man led us to a row of doors and opened one into our own private table. It had rose petals scattered on the table and was lit by the soft glow of candlelight. I looked around and quirked an eyebrow at him.

He blushed. "Apologies, ladies, these tables are normally kept for more romantic encounters. I told Jason to clear this out, but if you wait just a moment, I can take care of it."

He advanced toward the table, but I shot out my arm and stopped him short. "That's alright, we'll make do."

He blinked in surprise for a moment before recovering and saying, "If you're sure?"

Hollywood seemed to remember herself then, and moved away from me again to the table. He quickly followed her and pulled the chair out from the table for her with a flourish. "We're sure. It's perfect. Thank you, Antonio."

Of course she was on a first name basis with the staff here.

I moved to my chair and saw Antonio panic and saved him the internal struggle about whether he should pull out my chair, by waving my hand at him in a 'don't worry about it' gesture before pulling out my own chair and seating myself.

"Would you like the usual, Miss Hollywood, or would you like a menu?" he asked.

She giggled at that. "I'll probably take my usual, but Maya could use a menu if you wouldn't mind."

"Of course! I'll be right back," he said, rushing off.

I was grateful he had been too focused on her to notice me rolling my eyes at the jab. Of course she would assume I had never been here and would need to see a menu. She was right, but still. I glared at her but couldn't help noticing how her eyes looked darker in the candlelight. They were a bright blue normally, but the candlelight made them look much darker, deeper.

I was taken aback and felt my gaze soften.

A moment later, the waiter came back with a menu that he placed in front of me before leaving again. Although having a private room defeated the main purpose of our outing, it was a relief to not have to be on every second around her. It had been a while since I had taken such a demanding job, and while I knew I was up to the task, I was relieved they were easing us into it.

I looked down at the menu, not bothering to pay much attention to her, but the moment my eyes took in the prices, I had to force myself to keep breathing. I bit my tongue, forcing myself to not say something. How anyone could feel like any sort of food was worth these prices was beyond me. I was just glad I knew without having to ask that Hollywood would be paying. Thank goodness, because there was no way in hell I could afford this. At least not yet. Maybe once Elite cut me their check, it would be a different story. Once word got out that Hollywood and I were an item and I was relevant again and producers started knocking on my door again, maybe I could come back and eat here on my own dime. Maybe.

I glanced up at her over the menu and saw her watching me. "What's good here?" I asked, perusing the menu. Unsure how to decide what to pick, I was tempted to just order the most expensive thing on the menu and another one to go for later, but that would be showing Hollywood I cared about the place and was impressed by it. I wasn't sure I was willing to do that.

She shrugged. "It really doesn't matter what you pick. Everything's good here."

Of course she could say that with confidence. The undertone of arrogance coating her words made me resolve then and there to spend as much of her money tonight as I possibly could.

CHAPTER 14
SAVANNAH

I wanted to enjoy my dinner. I should be enjoying myself at my favorite restaurant, but sitting across from Maya, seeing the way she was eyeing the menu with disbelief, I couldn't bring myself to relax. She finally ordered a lobster dish I hadn't had the pleasure of trying yet, which happened to be the most expensive thing on the menu, surprise surprise.

I *was* surprised, though, when she ordered us both a glass of my favorite champagne. "How'd you know?" I asked. It had to be a coincidence. She couldn't have known that it was my favorite.

"Know what? Good champagne? I might not be a multi-millionaire like you, but I know good champagne." She was glaring at me, and I rolled my eyes.

She had a talent for misinterpreting everything I said. "I just meant it's my favorite."

She watched me before smirking. "Of course it is."

She continued watching me, and I couldn't help reaching for my phone out of instinct. I was anxious and wanted something to do, something to look at, but I remembered before I had moved too far that I didn't have my phone.

Clarice still had both of our phones and was monitoring and posting on our socials for us. Who knew what she was posting, but at least I knew Lexi was approving everything, so I didn't really have to worry. But I was still getting used to it. I felt naked without my phone, especially now.

Normally, I could scroll through my phone and not have to look at Maya, not have to sit in the awkwardness I was feeling, but that was exactly why Clarice did this. That was the whole point, to make us work through the uncomfortable moments. I just wished it felt remotely like Maya was trying to be on my side with this. I felt myself squirm in my chair as she continued to stare at me. When she saw that, she smirked. I hoped she was as uncomfortable as I was, but I doubted it. It was incredibly frustrating that she seemed to want to make this as difficult as possible for the both of us. Although, maybe I was being too harsh on her. She did order me champagne, and whether or not it was an accident, it was my favorite. So, it was something.

Antonio came back a moment later, and I had never been so happy to see someone in my life. He set the glasses on the table and, unfortunately, swiftly departed.

I turned my attention back to Maya, who had picked up a glass, and asked, "Should we toast?"

She quirked an eyebrow at me. "With what?"

Now it was my turn to be confused. "A champagne toast," I said slowly. "To the start of a wonderful partnership?" I asked, reaching for the other glass, but Maya reached it first.

"Maybe next time if you wanted to do a toast, you should have ordered something to drink," she said, bringing the glass to her lips and smirking. I watched in disbelief as she drank from the glass that should have been mine. Without thinking, I reached across the table for the other glass. I got my hand around it but not quickly enough since she got her other hand around it before I could move the glass. She quickly put her original glass down and glared at me. "What the hell do you think you're doing?" she gritted out.

"Me? You're the one trying to double fist champagne expensive enough to support a family of four for a month."

Her eyes flashed with anger and her grip tightened on the glass we were both holding. "You're just mad you didn't think to order some."

"I'm just mad I thought for a second that you would think about anyone besides yourself."

"Talk about pot calling the kettle. When have you ever thought about anyone besides yourself? You haven't changed a bit, Hollywood. Still toxic as ever."

I couldn't believe her. "I'm hardly the toxic one." I pulled the glass closer to me.

She looked surprised and yanked it back in her direction. "You're really gonna fight me for it?"

I narrowed my eyes. I could just order my own, but she made this personal, and I refused to let her win.

I yanked the glass back in my direction at the same time that she tried to pull it closer to her; she was stronger and I could only watch as she pulled it out of my grip, sending the champagne careening toward her. Champagne spilled all over her shirt. I felt a mix of horror and satisfaction seeing her looking down in disbelief at the spreading liquid.

She looked up, eyes narrowed. "You did that on purpose!"

"As if! It's not my fault you're too strong."

"If you hadn't fought me for it, this wouldn't have happened."

If she wanted to find someone to blame, I would make damn sure she knew where the blame should really fall. "If you'd been a proper date and ordered me a glass, too, this wouldn't have happened."

"If this was a real date, I might have."

"If this was a real date, I would've left already."

I looked down to see how bad it was, and saw her white shirt was basically see through. It was clinging to her dark green bra that I could make out clearly through the white of her top. I was surprised by how lacy her bra was. A lot more lace than I would have thought. I wondered if that was her decision or if it was Miss Lucy's styling.

I looked back up and saw she was glaring at me, but a moment later, her look turned mischievous. "If this was a real date, I would think my date did that on purpose."

"Why would anyone do that on purpose?" I asked, crossing my arms.

"Why would my date want to get me wet?" she asked, gesturing to her shirt, causing me to blush redder than the rose petals on the table.

I couldn't help my eyes from dropping to her shirt again. Her breasts were straining against the fabric and the chill of the champagne had made her nipples harden. I struggled to tear my eyes away, wondering what it would feel like to touch her.

She cleared her throat, and guiltily my eyes shot up to meet hers, my blush deepening.

"I would assume she was in a real rush to get me undressed. In fact, I might just give her a sneak peek," she said, and my eyes tracked her movements as she slowly reached down and grabbed hold of her shirt.

I couldn't pry my eyes from her if I tried, but I sure as hell wasn't trying. She raised her shirt further, and I held my breath. I watched the fabric trail over her skin, exposing her lower stomach, higher and higher, until I could see the very edge of her bra.

"Enjoying the show, Hollywood?"

I gulped, but my eyes didn't leave her hands, and I stayed silent. *What the hell was wrong with me?* I couldn't tear my eyes from her newly exposed skin. I wanted to see more, I wanted to lick it. *There was seriously something wrong with me.*

She cleared her throat and my eyes shot to hers. "I asked you a question. Are you enjoying the show?"

I blushed. She had me mesmerized, and she knew it. I wanted to deny it, wanted to be strong and not give her the satisfaction, but I wasn't that good of an actress. I couldn't hide how she was making me feel, so there was no use lying. I nodded.

"Uh, uh, uh," she said, shaking her head, and slowly lowered her shirt a fraction of an inch. I whimpered in frustration and she let out a breathy laugh before saying, "I want to hear you say it."

"Yes," I uttered, knowing I would regret it later, but not able to bring myself to care.

She quirked an eyebrow at me and raised her shirt a fraction of an inch more, exposing the underside of her bra again. In that moment, I knew I was under her spell. There wasn't anything I wouldn't do to see more of her.

"Yes, what?"

"Yes, I'm enjoying it," I forced out, "Happy?" I couldn't help adding.

She grinned. "Maybe, but drop the attitude or the show stops."

I bit my lip and saw her eyes track the motion. A moment later, she returned her focus back to my eyes and said, "Well, Hollywood, what happens next is up to you. Tell me what you want."

Well, I have already gotten this far. Fuck it, I might as well keep going. "You know what I want," I told her.

"But I want to hear you say it. Be a good girl and tell me."

She was asking too much, taking too much from me. "No," I said, shaking my head.

"No?" she asked, and I watched her lower her shirt a bit more again.

"Wait," I said, sounding desperate and hating it.

She grinned. "Wait, what?"

"What do you want from me?" I asked, almost begging now.

"Be a good girl and tell me what you want."

A shiver ran up my spine at that, and I felt the heat rush to my core.

"Come on, Hollywood, tell me what you want."

"Take off your shirt," I ground out, warring with myself and losing. I knew this was a bad idea, a terrible one, but I needed to see more of her.

She lifted her shirt, exposing her bra. The jade green lacy bra made me suck in a breath. It was see through, hiding nothing. Her hardened nipples were on full display. I was so enraptured by her, I almost didn't hear her say, "Good girl," but my body reacted to it, to her. I felt the heat rush to my core. Before I could stop myself, I clenched my thighs together and bit my lip. I didn't take my eyes off her, and she didn't stop there. As I watched, she pulled her shirt completely over her head. When she had it all the way off, she balled it up. "Much better, wouldn't you say?" she asked, winking at me before throwing it at me. "I'm much more comfortable now."

I felt myself blushing. I threw her shirt to the floor and watched her pick up her unspilled glass of champagne and take a sip. She moved the glass from her lips and ran her tongue along it.

I was still watching her when Antonio came back with our dinner. I felt the heat rush to my face and knew it was flushed a deep crimson.

If Antonio was surprised by Maya's state of undress, he recovered too quickly to show it. In addition to our food, he had brought a couple more glasses of champagne.

"On the house," he said with a flourish. "Your favorite, of course." He grinned at me and I smiled back at him. He seemed to be avoiding looking at Maya. I was impressed at how professional and respectful he was being.

"Thank you so much, Antonio. You're too kind."

"Yes, too kind. My girlfriend really appreciates it," Maya said. I blushed deeper and watched as he looked at her. In an effort of massive proportions, his eyes only dipped lower than her face for a moment. How he managed that, I don't know. "And I appreciate anything that makes my baby girl happy."

He turned back to me and said, "Apologies, ladies. I didn't know you were both spoken for."

"I'm still getting used to it myself," I said honestly.

Maya laughed and said, "She's so shy. Isn't it adorable? I'll have her unlocking her wild side soon enough, though," she said with a mischievous grin that sent a shiver down my spine.

I knew this was an act, but for a moment, just a breath, I wanted to believe it. I wanted to believe that this woman would ravish me the moment Antonio left, wanted to believe that there was something between us, wanted to forget our awful past and just enjoy the way this beautiful woman was looking at me.

Antonio ducked out, and we were alone again.

"I think we need some rules," she said, considering.

I didn't love the sound of that. "What do you mean?"

"Clarice is always talking about boundaries and communication, so some rules, to make sure we understand each other."

That didn't sound so bad, although I'm sure there was more to it than that.

"Okay..." I said, hesitantly. "What do you have in mind?"

"Rule one. If we're going to really sell this, then you are *mine*. You're spoken for and if I find you flirting with anyone again the way you were with *Antonio* there will be consequences."

"Flirting? Me? With Antonio? I wasn't flirting with him!"

"Either you were flirting with him or you throw yourself at everyone you talk to, but if you keep it up, there will be consequences."

The way she looked at me when she said that sent my brain haywire. I couldn't think and felt my whole body heat. "Consequences? What consequences?"

"That's for me to know and you to worry about," she said, smirking. "In fact, I think you owe me."

I gulped. "I do?"

She looked thoughtful a moment before nodding decisively. "Yes, yes, you do. I don't know what type of relationships you've been in before, but you don't flirt with someone in front of your girlfriend. Apologize."

What the hell. "No. I wasn't even flirting with him."

"Well, if you're going to be a bad girl and not apologize, I'm going to have to do something about it."

I felt a thrill run through my body at that, and I hated that she was able to make me feel this way. I hated her, but damn if she wasn't sexy as hell, especially in that lacy bra that left nothing to the imagination.

She picked up her glass and sashayed over to me. I was still sitting. I thought for a moment maybe I should stand, be level with her, but before I could move, she pushed my chair back from the table and straddled me. She snaked her free arm behind my head, keeping her champagne in hand between us. She shifted herself closer until she was only inches and a champagne glass from me. I felt her body press against mine for a moment and wondered what it would feel like if I were wearing less.

She pressed her chest against mine and I fought the urge to reach out and touch her, and somehow found the strength to keep looking her in the eyes and not let my eyes sink lower. Her hand behind my head tilted my face up to meet hers. I felt the butterflies in my stomach at that, full of anticipation, craving her kiss. She moved her lips closer to mine, but stopped a breath from me and whispered, "Open."

Without hesitation, I opened my mouth for her. To my disappointment, she moved back, and the glass met my lips. She tipped the glass to my lips and slowly tilted the liquid to me, but before any hit my tongue, she moved the glass back. "Don't swallow. If you swallow the fun stops, understood?"

I nodded, and she tilted the glass to me again. The champagne coated my tongue and the sweet flavor started to fill my mouth. She slowed her pour. "What a good girl, dying to impress me."

All my focus was on trying not to swallow and the sensation of the bubbles against my tongue.

Just when I thought I couldn't take anymore, she stopped. I quickly closed my mouth, but I still didn't swallow. She watched me, waiting, for what I didn't know.

A moment passed, and another. The bubbles danced on my tongue and she was undressing me with her eyes. With mine, I was pleading with her to let me swallow.

I didn't know what the hell had gotten into me, but there was something about how she called me a good girl that made me desperate to hear it again.

She licked my lips with her tongue and a soft moan escaped me as I fought not to swallow, to obey her.

She leaned back again, and I pouted, as much as I could with my mouth full. She laughed and leaned back closer to me. "Good girls share. You're a good girl, aren't you, baby?"

I nodded quickly, feeling the champagne slosh around my mouth. "Are you going to share with me?"

I nodded, pleading with my eyes.

"Prove it," she said.

That was all I needed to hear. I closed the distance between us and crashed my lips onto hers.

CHAPTER 15

MAYA

Her mouth was so full of champagne she had to swallow a little to make room for my tongue. I lapped up some of the champagne, reveling in the delicious taste of her mingled with the champagne. Our tongues danced and I felt the bubbles hitting my tongue. Champagne had never tasted so sweet.

When the champagne was gone too soon, I kissed her a little more before pulling away.

The whimper she let out when my lips left hers almost made me go back for more. Almost. But I stayed strong. I was calling the shots and the sooner she figured that out, the better. There would be plenty of time for me to enjoy her little noises if I played this right. "Rule two, you listen to me. I'm calling the shots."

I saw an argument rising in her and booped her on the nose. "The choice is yours, baby girl, but if you don't do what I say, the fun stops."

I didn't know if I was bluffing or not, so I hoped she didn't call me out. I wanted this as badly as she did. Probably worse. I hadn't dreamed of taking things this far, but I loved seeing Hollywood begging for me. There was something intoxicating about having her under my control. That's what it was, I just loved being in control. My burning desire was more for the situation than for her, I reasoned. I was dominating a beautiful woman, that's what was driving me, not any special desire for her. Even as I tried to convince myself, I wasn't sure I believed it.

Hollywood still looked dazed. I ran my thumb over her swollen lip, waiting, and she nodded.

"Uh, uh" I said, instantly pulling away my thumb. "Say it."

She looked at me pleadingly, but I didn't relent. I could see the confusion, the need, and her stubbornness warring across her face. If I was right about her, the need would win. I hoped I was right. I needed to be right.

"Okay."

"Okay what?" I said, moving my thumb back to trace her lip.

"Okay, I'll listen to you. Now get the hell back over here and kiss me."

As much as I wanted to, that wasn't how this was going to work. She already had all the power here. She had the power to ruin me professionally. And with the little noises she made, I was starting to think she might have the power to ruin me personally, and I couldn't have that. So, she would play by my rules.

"Not so fast. I'm calling the shots." I took her glass of champagne from the table behind me and took a sip, just enough to assert my claim. She watched me, so I took my time savoring the sip, closing my eyes and moaning, putting on a good show for her. When I opened my eyes, hers were still glued to me. I savored that for a moment before asking, "Do you want some more?"

She nodded quickly; I knew she was lost in the feeling since she didn't even bother to ask whether I meant more of me or of the champagne. Her eyes told me she didn't care which, she just needed more. Craved more, and I wouldn't be the one to deny her.

I tipped the glass to her lips, spilling a little liquid into her mouth before moving quicker than she could stop me and pouring the rest on her chest. Champagne flowed down the top of her dress and spilling down into her cleavage. Her breasts glistening were a sight to behold.

She inhaled sharply. "What the hell?" she said, looking betrayed and glaring at me.

I shrugged, using a finger to wipe the last of the champagne from her lips before tracing my finger down the curve of her neck. She leaned into me.

"You thought I forgot about earlier?" I asked, grinning. "I wasn't going to be the only one getting wet today."

"You weren't," she half-whispered, half-whimpered so quietly if it wasn't for her blush, I wouldn't have been sure I heard her right.

"Well, sweetheart, why don't we do something about that? Get you a little more comfortable." I slid my fingers up to her thin dress straps and slid a finger under each, lifting them slightly. I watched her, waiting for her to stop me, to say or do anything that implied she wanted me to stop. I wasn't sure how far I could push her, but I felt like she would come to her senses at any moment. To my shock and excitement, she didn't stop me.

I slowly slid the straps to the edges of her shoulders, watching, waiting, but nothing. I held my breath as I pushed them off her shoulders, one at a time. Slowly waiting to see if she would tell me to stop, but she didn't The straps fell away, and as if it snapped her out of her daze, her hands rushed to cover herself. I grabbed one of her hands, letting her have the other to hold up her dress. It was enough to keep it from slipping, but just barely. The top of her strapless bra was peeking out. I let my fingers trace the outline of her bra, dipping for a moment into her glistening cleavage, still slick from the champagne.

"What are we doing?" she said out loud.

"Having some fun," I answered. Bringing her other hand to the back of my head and lacing it in my hair, making her look at me, I brought my hand, still slick from the champagne on her chest, to my lips and sucked the champagne from my fingers. She watched me, mesmerized. When I was done, I asked, "Is that re-

ally what you want to be doing with your other hand?"
I asked.

She took another look at me and whispered, "No."
"Show me."

That was all she needed. She let go of her dress and closed the little distance between us, pressing her lips to mine. She was more forceful this time, really getting into it. She pressed her chest against mine. I could feel my breasts straining against my lace bra. I wanted to get a good look at her chest now that her dress wasn't completely covering her, but I couldn't bring myself to part from her lips. I jumped in surprise when I felt her hand slip in between us and slide over the lace covering my breasts. I shivered as she passed over my nipple. Good to know Hollywood didn't waste any time. This was going to be fun.

I pulled away and kissed her neck, working my way down. I was wondering how far she would let me go when I heard the sobering noise of the door clicking open and a soft little gasp come from Hollywood's lips.

In a few quick movements, I pulled her dress up and pulled her to me, covering her and giving her time to collect herself.

I slowly turned, careful not to expose her further. Yes, Hollywood could use a good scandal and deserved to be taken down a few pegs, but not this way. I wouldn't cross that line. I saw the waiter staring at us and I grinned back, saying, "Apologies, me and my girlfriend have some *pressing* business that has to be attended to. If you wouldn't mind wrapping up our dinner, we'll be taking it to go."

"Certainly, ladies. My apologies. I'll be back in a moment."

With that, he quickly left the room, and I heard Hollywood let out a sigh. I turned around and saw what I expected, but was still disappointed that she had covered herself back up. "That was close. What the hell even was that?"

"That was you showing me you have a wild side. Who knew Hollywood had an exhibitionist streak?"

The look of outrage on her face was enough to tell me we were probably back to pretending there was nothing between us, pretending that didn't just happen and that anything that did happen between us was just for show, for our contracts, but I knew differently. Hollywood's body responded to me, and she had a submissive streak that I would be damned if I didn't explore further.

"What?" she exclaimed. "No, I don't!"

I grinned, watching her as I slowly ground my hips into hers, feeling her buck against me. "Look at how you respond to me. I know you, Hollywood. You're getting off on this."

She blushed so hard her neck reddened. I ran my tongue up her neck, right to her ear, and lightly sucked on her earlobe. I heard her moan and pulled back.

"Face it, you're enjoying this. You love that anyone could walk in at any second."

She looked conflicted, but shook her head.

"Yes, you do. You love that I'm taking control, love that you agreed to do what I say. You love that I'm in charge. In fact, why don't you undo your straps and show me what I was too busy to enjoy before?"

She paused a moment, biting her lip, looking unsure, but her hands were on her straps. "What if he comes back?"

"What if he does?" I asked, unconcerned. "He seemed to be flirting with you pretty hard. I'm sure he'd enjoy the show."

Her blush deepened, but she didn't move. I leaned closer to her and whispered in her ear, "Maybe he'd want to join us."

I felt a shove at my chest and moved back, seeing her glaring at me.

"I don't know what the hell got into me, but I can promise you it won't happen again. Whatever little games you think you're playing, knock them the hell off. They aren't working. From now on, we're keeping things professional. If there's no one around to see, I don't want you touching me. Get off me."

I wasn't surprised in the slightest that she was pulling back already. Of course giving me any sort of power over her would scare her. Poor Hollywood always had to be the one in charge, the one calling the shots. I never imagined she would have a secret submissive side, but now that I knew, our relationship, fake or not, was going to be a lot more fun. I moved from her lap, reluctantly giving her the distance she asked for.

"Of course, because it's only fun for you when people are watching. I understand.

She groaned and threw her hands up in the air. "That's not what I meant and you know it!"

I smirked at her. I had to admit she was adorable when she was frustrated. I grabbed my shirt from the floor and was pleasantly surprised to see it had mostly dried. I looked at Hollywood and saw she wasn't so lucky. Her pink dress was almost see-through with the damp stain on the front.

"Sure it isn't," I said with a wink. "Just know that you've been a bad girl today. You promised to listen to me and you didn't, so no matter how much you beg me to touch you tonight, you're going to have to make do with your own fingers."

She blushed crimson and took a minute to say, "As if I'd ask that of you, or do that with you in the room."

I hadn't even thought about the fact that we shared a room, but the fact that she had, and had pictured the scenario for a moment, made me grin. "No matter where you do it, it's enough to know you'll be thinking of me."

The waiter reappeared before she could say anything else, packaged up our dinners, and informed us the tab had already been paid for and that our ride was waiting for us. She wouldn't meet my eye, and much to my amusement, she was looking with concern at the front of her dress.

I couldn't help rubbing salt in her wound. "I would offer you my jacket, but, unfortunately, only good girls get to borrow my jacket."

She glared at me, and threw her shoulders back, standing tall. "Like I'd ever borrow something that had touched you."

I rolled my eyes at that. She was so quick to forget how eager she just was to touch me. She stormed out of the room, and I followed quickly. It wouldn't be good for us if she was seen looking that exposed and pissed off. As funny as it would be, I couldn't let her. Besides, the press would have a field day about her wearing my jacket.

I caught up to her in the hall, holding my jacket out to her, and whispered, "Suit yourself. I'm sure the restaurant and half the world would love to see those beautiful tits of yours."

She turned, glaring at me, saw the jacket I was offering, and looked conflicted. "Wear my jacket. I'd rather be the only one to see your chest tonight."

She snatched the jacket out of my hands and put it on quickly, grumbling, "I didn't show you anything."

I came up behind her and pulled her back into me, hugging her tight around her waist. I leaned to her ear and whispered, "Yes, but you would have, and I can't wait for the moment you do." With that, I let go of her and tapped her on the ass, pushing her forward. She remembered herself and started to move again, and I quickly followed.

Chapter 16

Savannah

Clarice was overjoyed to see me in Maya's jacket, until the moment we were in the car with the doors shut and I peeled it off quickly, like I was worried it was going to give me a rash.

She saw the stain on my shirt and just groaned; she didn't ask what happened, which I was grateful for. I hardly knew what to think myself about what happened, never mind how to explain it to her.

Maya wouldn't stop smirking at me. At least someone was happy, I thought bitterly. That was the first and last time that was going to happen. That much, I was sure of.

But if I was so sure, why was it her I was thinking of when I was curled up in bed that night with only the mountain of pillows separating us? Why did I have the urge for a moment to fling myself across the pillow barrier and lay with her?

I was lonely. That had to be it. I hadn't had time to date or be close to anyone lately and she scratched an itch for me. Satisfied a need my body had. That was it, because that had to be all it was. I didn't like her;

I didn't even trust her. I wouldn't let my guard down with her again. I couldn't.

A HOLLYWOOD HIGH HOMECOMING?!

Spotted last night out together were none other than Hollywood High alumni, the infamous frenemies, Savannah Hollywood and Maya Ryder.

This reporter saw them walking arm in arm into Rizzo's, looking closer than ever.

Has hell frozen over, or have Savannah and Maya squashed their feud enough to befriends? Could there be a Hollywood High Reunion on the horizon? Could we finally get the series closure we all craved?

Perhaps even more interesting was their choice in location. Could Savannah have been introducing her old friend to her new beau? It's long been rumored that the Hollywood starlet has been slumming it with a Rizzo's waiter. The very same waiter was spotted escorting her and Maya back to their car. Savannah was trying to disguise herself by wearing Maya's jacket, but she couldn't fool us.

We have exclusive photos of Savannah's new beau waving her and Maya off as they made their escape.

We can't help asking ourselves why Savannah's trying so hard to keep her new beau a secret and when she'll come out with the truth.

One thing's for sure, when the truth comes out, we'll be right on the front lines to report it to you.

Chapter 17

Savannah

Clarice had slapped the paper down in front of us that morning. The headline had surprised me, to be honest. I was expecting something about me and Maya. I was thinking there would be speculation, especially when I glimpsed the picture of me wearing her jacket further down on the page, but as I read it, I found myself getting more and more annoyed.

Even when I was trying to use the press to my advantage, trying to get them to notice me and who I was 'dating', they couldn't get it right. When I got to the part about me supposedly dating Antonio, I slammed down my copy, scowling at it.

Maya, who had been reading over my shoulder, laughed.

I whipped around. "What's so funny?"

She gestured at the paper. "The reporter agrees he was totally flirting with you."

"Ugh!" I groaned loudly. "For the last time, he wasn't flirting with me! He's nice to me because it's his job!"

She was still laughing, so I turned back to Clarice. "I know we were going to wait a little longer, but I'm doing it tonight."

Maya stopped laughing, and Clarice tilted her head, considering. "During the interview?" she asked.

I nodded. "I know the interview's supposed to be about the album and the paparazzi was going to catch us in a compromising position in a couple of days, but I'm starting to think they still won't get it." I groaned. "They never see or report what I want them to, and besides, I want a chance to speak for myself. I have something I want to say."

After all, I was giving all of myself to the world yet again. I regularly did so through my music, but this was different. I was exposing a new truth, a new deeply hidden part of me, and for once I wanted to be in control of when and how my own story was told.

Maya put her hand on my shoulder, making me jump before shrugging it off.

"Are you sure that's a good idea?" Maya asked. Whether she was asking me or Clarice, I didn't know. Was I sure? Not at all, but I knew I was going to do it, regardless.

"Think about it, Clare," I said, begging, "It's the first interview since we announced the album. It's the prime time. Besides, they're definitely going to ask about Darren's lies. I'm going to get slaughtered if I don't say something, and it's my moment, I should have a say in it."

She sighed and said, "Okay, I'm not saying yes, but I'm not saying no either. I'll make some calls and see what I can do."

I nodded, knowing there was only so much she could do. My contract was pretty iron clad and if Elite didn't agree to it, I would have to stay silent for now. I knew Clarice was doing her best navigating between me and Elite, and I appreciated it. I knew Elite had my best interests at heart. I paid them well enough to make sure of it. The look Clarice was giving me told me she understood, but I needed to make sure she knew how important this was to me. "Thank you. I don't want to have to be strong and stay silent tonight. I want to be able to be myself."

She took hold of my hand in both of hers and nodded. "I understand, honey. I'll do my best."

With that, she hurried out of the room, already dialing, leaving me to sit around anxiously hoping and counting the minutes.

CHAPTER 18

MAYA

If I didn't know better, I would think she was actually scared, but there was no way. Everyone loved her, regardless of what she did. I learned that the hard way long ago when I tried to tell the world how she burned me and no one had any sympathy for me. I was made into an outcast and she was portrayed as the victim.

That always happened, but sitting there with her, I couldn't deny that her anxiety was real. Seeing her squirm reminded me of how I had felt as a young queer kid in Hollywood, and I hated myself for it, but I started to feel some pity for her. Maybe it was just the memory of her lips on mine, or maybe I was going soft. Either way, I wasn't thrilled with the development.

I groaned, surrendering to my impulses, and took a seat on the couch next to her. I waited for her to look at me, but she didn't. I finally put my hand on her chin and turned her head to look at me.

Seeing the worry in her eyes made me swallow hard. I hadn't looked her in the eye since we left the restaurant. I had been keeping my distance, but I couldn't leave her alone right now, not in this.

"You know it's going to be fine. Everyone loves you."

She looked more worried. "Exactly. They love the me I've been pretending to be. They love the girl who has a new guy every month. They love the heartbreaker, the girl who jumps from guy to guy, the girl whose love life they can always speculate on. What if they don't love me? The real me."

"Ah, come on," I joked. "They're still going to speculate. There's just more possibilities now."

When her face fell, it was clear that was the exact wrong thing to say. "You're right," she said. "They're never going to leave me alone."

"That's not really such a bad thing, is it?" I asked, genuine curiosity getting the better of me. I would kill for people to care about me the way her fans did.

She looked at me wide eyed. "You're kidding, right?"

I wasn't.

"You wouldn't get it," she said, waving her hand dismissively.

I pulled away from her in an instant, already regretting the ounce of pity I had been feeling for her. I jumped up from the couch, crossing my arms.

"Of course I don't. It must be so freaking hard being you. Everyone's always fawning all over you, fighting for the newest exclusive. Everyone can't wait to find out the latest and greatest about you. Your fans are always talking about who you're dating. Your fans are always talking about you. Even people who aren't fans of yours have at least heard of you. It must be really fucking hard. Some difficult life you have there, Hollywood."

She turned to look at me, shocked, and I was surprised to see anger matching my own flash in her eyes. "You don't fucking get it. Yes, my fans are phenomenal, but the world is always there, watching, judging, waiting for me to slip up. I'm walking a tightrope with no safety net. What do you think happens to me if I slip up?"

"Nothing! And that's my goddamn point. You're a superstar! You're untouchable, and you want to come to me about your problems? Cry me a river."

"You don't get it. This is all I have. All that I am. Who the hell is Savannah Hollywood without her fans? If tomorrow all of this was taken away from me, sure I'd still be okay physically, but I would have nothing. Without my job, without my fans, I'm nothing but a sad, single thirty-year-old divorcee whose only friends are her manager and her band. I am constantly bending over backwards trying to impress my fans, trying to make sure they still love me, that they don't turn their backs on me, because without this, I have nothing. Without this, I am nothing. If this plan fails, if people don't believe me that I'm a bisexual woman, or that we're dating, if they think for a goddamn second that I'm lying to them all about my sexuality or about my relationships, I'm going to be massacred."

That hit harder than I wanted it to. I knew she had never been close with her family, but hearing she only had Lexi and her band for friends made my heart ache for her. I pushed the feeling as far down as I could and instead said, "Boo hoo. So what if your fans turn on you? You're still worth millions more than I'll ever be."

She deflated. She didn't look angry anymore, just tired. "I'm sorry," she said.

Sure she was. She was a superstar and got everything we had ever dreamed of without me, at my expense, but she was sorry. Like that fixed a goddamn thing.

"Save it," was all I said.

She looked up at me, examining the anger on my face, like she was thinking about saying more, but Clarice came back in.

Clarice looked more frazzled than I had ever seen her, but she put on a smile and walked over to Hollywood. She put her hand on Hollywood's shoulder and said, "So, do you know what you're going to say?"

She took a moment to look up at Clarice. There was hope burning in Savannah's eyes. "Really? You mean it?"

I could still feel the stress radiating from Clarice and knew this couldn't have at all been an easy task. Hollywood was shining with gratitude and threw her arms around Clarice, squealing, "Thank you! Thank you! Thank you!"

Clarice hugged her back and chuckled, patting her on the back. "Yeah, yeah, just don't make me regret this, kid."

Hollywood was still smiling when she pulled back, but her smile didn't hide the doubt in her eyes. For our sakes and the sake of my paycheck, I hoped she knew what she was getting into.

Chapter 19

SAVANNAH

I took a deep breath. I could do this. I was standing alone, waiting. Connor, Stevie, and Nikki were still getting ready. They didn't have to be on stage for a little while longer. The show wanted us to perform earlier, but I needed to get this out of the way first, before I chickened out.

The plan was simple; I was going to tell the truth. Well, most of it. I was going to tell my side about what happened with Darren, and then tell them about a new whirlwind romance, play one of my love songs and ask the audience if they want to meet her, listen to them go wild, and then bring out Maya. I could do this. I was scared, but my fans would support me. They had to, because I didn't know what I would do if they didn't. I couldn't lose the only thing about my life that still made sense. Darren took so much from me when he walked away; my plans for the future, the only family I had ever really been a part of, my belief in love, and my happiness. I wouldn't let him take my calling from me.

I took another deep breath and was surprised to feel warm fingers lace themselves in between mine.

I looked over, expecting to see Connor or Stevie had slipped over to check on me. They didn't know the scope of what I was sharing today, but they knew I was anxious about talking about my divorce. I figured one of them might have snuck away to wish me luck, but it wasn't either of them. I almost let go when I saw it was Maya before remembering myself and where we were. Of course she wanted to be seen supporting me.

She squeezed my hand gently, running her thumb over my hand. Instinctually, I leaned into her. She brushed my hair behind my ear with her free hand, leaning closer, putting her lips to my ear, and whispered, "Don't get the wrong idea, Hollywood."

I flinched and started to pull away, but she pulled me closer to her. She sighed before saying, "No one deserves to have to come out alone, and since you're not really in a position to have told your friends what you're doing, I figured..." She shrugged, letting her sentence trail off.

"Figured what?" I asked, confused by the rare glimpse behind her mask I was getting. It wasn't often that I saw her at a loss for words, and I guessed that was the case for most of the people in her life.

"Figured you could use support."

I exhaled softly and felt the beginnings of a tentative smile cross my face. She was doing me a kindness, queer kid to queer kid, and I couldn't help thinking maybe there was hope for our friendship after all. The thought gave me the little bit of courage I needed and I was grateful to her for it. "Thank you."

They called me out before anything else could be said. Before I moved, she squeezed my hand again, saying softly, "Give 'em hell, Hollywood."

I grinned. When I moved away from her and walked onto the stage, I told myself the flush of my cheeks was from the stage lights.

I was getting frustrated and, not for the first time, wondered what Lexi and Clarice would do if I just walked off stage. We were in front of a live audience who seemed to be eating up Teresa's monologue, but I was sick of it. I was starting to think Darren put her up to this. Lexi promised me she vetted the show and the audience and that they were the most likely to be sympathetic, but Teresa had been going on about how rough Darren has had it lately, being left by America's Sweetheart.

It was the weirdest interview I had done to date, since she seemed to only be talking to herself and the audience. She hadn't taken much input from me or even paid me much attention. I had lost control of the situation and didn't know what to do. The band was scheduled to come out shortly, so at least that would save me, but until then I didn't know how to get this interview back on track.

CHAPTER 20

MAYA

Watching from the wings was frustrating. This was taking way longer than we planned. She should have come out by now. *Was she chickening out?* I wondered for a moment before dismissing it.

I was antsy, and it didn't help that the host was being downright bitchy to her. *Wasn't she supposed to be on Hollywood's payroll?* They told me she picked this show because the host would be sympathetic, but clearly, they were wrong. The host was singing her ex's praises and trashing Hollywood.

For the first couple of minutes, it was a little vindicating to hear someone else hating on America's Sweetheart, but then she kept going. As I watched, Hollywood seemed to shrink in her seat, making herself smaller. I should have felt amused, but the sight made me sick. It was only then that Teresa finally addressed her.

"Everyone here knows how wonderful Darren is. Anyone here would have felt lucky to be in your shoes, to have his love, so tell me, what makes you think you're better than him?"

"I... I-" she stuttered.

It was painful to watch. I looked around for Lexi or Clarice, or even her band. Where the hell were they, anyway? Someone needed to march out there and put a stop to this, save her. She was being massacred out there.

"Why did you leave him, Savannah?"

"I-"

My feet started moving before I realized what I was doing I was doing. Her eyes whipped over to mine and the fear in them more than anything made me sure this was the right decision.

"She left him for me," I said loudly enough that Teresa's head whipped over to me and I saw the anger on her face that whatever weird interrogation she was doing had been interrupted. Good. Only when the audience gasped did I notice I was standing next to one of the stage microphones.

Well, I'm already on stage, better put on a show.

I crossed the stage and plopped down on the couch with Hollywood. I noticed smugly that she instinctually moved closer to me. Either she was a better actress than I gave her credit for, which was unlikely, but possible, or she was relieved I had rescued her.

I took her hand in mine and squeezed it. I was nothing if not committed.

Teresa had fixed her face, but the saccharine smile was somehow more off-putting than her glaring at me. After a moment of staring back at her, with the audience so quiet you could hear a pin drop, she asked, "Do I know you?"

I felt myself tense before feeling Hollywood's hand squeeze mine. I took a deep breath. Hollywood was right. I refused to let Teresa get to me.

"I would hope so. Maya Ryder, my darling Sav's old costar. Isn't that right, love?"

Hollywood just blinked at me. I squeezed her hand a little harder than I meant to, judging by her yelp, but she turned to Teresa and said, "Maya and I ran Hollywood High together."

I could see the gears turning in Teresa's head before it clicked. "Didn't you two hate each other?"

I laughed, nudging Hollywood to join me like it was an inside joke. "You could say we were passionate about each other. I used to think I hated her for stealing the show, but it turns out the show wasn't the only thing she stole..."

I paused for a moment, for dramatic effect and to look lovingly into Hollywood's eyes, but when I saw the panic start to overcome her face, I quickly finished. "She stole my heart."

There was a chorus of "awwwws" from the crowd, but Teresa didn't look amused. "Really?" was all she said.

Of course, now she had nothing to say. She was supposed to be the one asking the questions, and Hollywood hadn't said a damn thing either. Guess I was the one running the show now.

"Sav and I were waiting for the right time to tell the world, but after hearing how angry everyone is with her for following her heart, I couldn't hold my tongue. Sav and I were just kids when we started working together. I don't think either of us really understood our feelings for each other." I chuckled to myself. "I certainly didn't. I thought I hated poor Sav here. Clearly, I was wrong." I laughed again and was encouraged when the audience did, too. "I'm the luckiest woman in the world that she forgave me for how I acted toward her when we were young. I don't know how I got lucky enough to have such a strong, beautiful, self-assured, kind, and caring woman fall for me, too."

She smiled at me in a way that I knew was melting the audience's hearts. Even mine fluttered a little against my will.

Teresa cleared her throat. The glare she gave me made me stop talking for long enough for her to ask the audience, "You all don't buy this, do you?"

I held my breath for a moment, but the crowd cheered and then a call came through the cheers. One by one everyone started to pick up and join in, "Kiss her, kiss her, kiss her."

Fuck.

I should have expected that, but for some reason I hadn't. We should have planned for this. I mean, hell, I didn't even know if Hollywood was okay with this. I mean yes, we had kissed before, but this was different. This was so much more public.

A glance at her showed her biting her lip and looking back and forth between my eyes and my lips. She was blushing, but as much shit as I gave her to the contrary, she was actually a good actress, so I couldn't tell if it was okay, if she wanted this. I was hesitating, apparently too long for her since in a flash she closed the distance and her lips were on mine.

It was electric. I felt my body heating up as her lips tasted mine. I barely suppressed a groan when she slipped her tongue into my mouth.

The audience was going wild, but it wasn't until Teresa's voice broke through that I realized we were getting a little carried away. "Alright, alright ladies, enough already. This isn't that kind of show."

I pulled away quickly, a blush involuntarily coming over my face. I tried to put some distance between Hollywood and myself, but she nuzzled up closer to me.

Looking out at the camera and the audience, she said, "The truth is, Darren and I weren't right for each other. There's a lot that can be said about our relationship, but the truth is it wasn't right for us, either of us. There was a big part of myself that I had been hiding for much longer than I should, but Maya here helped me to see how important it is to be true to yourself. She opened my heart back up to the possibilities and opened my mind up to being honest with myself. I'm bisexual. No, I didn't cheat on Darren, but we did grow apart. It wasn't anyone's fault, but we fell out of love, or at least I did. It wasn't until Maya waltzed back into my life that I felt that spark of what was missing in my marriage."

At that, she turned to me with a look that made my heart do a backflip. "You brought me back to life and made me believe in love again. It feels like everything in my life was leading me to you."

The audience broke out in "awwww"s and my cheeks heated.

Under my breath, I whispered, "Laying it on a bit thick there, Hollywood."

She just grinned, and the audience was watching me expectantly.

I hesitated. We hadn't rehearsed this, so I wasn't sure what to say. There was something about her confession and the way she was looking at me that had me flushed. My throat was so dry I wasn't sure I could force words to come out if I tried.

My breath caught on what to say, something, anything. She was watching me. I had to say something., but before I could stumble over something and try to make myself sound smooth, Connor rushed onto stage with the rest of the band.

"So, it looks like the cat's out of the bag, huh?" he asked with a grin.

Hollywood gaped at him. "You knew?"

Liar. There's no way in hell her straight best friend knew before I did. For god's sake, I'm gay and it was a surprise to me.

He nodded. I narrowed my eyes at him for a moment before remembering where we were and losing the glare.

The band took their places, and she leaned into me, kissing me on the cheek chastely, like she hadn't had her tongue down my throat a few minutes ago.

"Sing your heart out, Hollywood." I meant to say it quietly, but judging by the cheers, they all heard.

That night I found myself lying awake staring at the ceiling, thinking about her performance. She really put on a show, both singing and with me. Once she recovered out there, she put on an Oscar worthy performance.

That was the real reason I gave her as much crap as I did about acting. Singing had always been her thing, acting was mine. I hated that she might be better than me at that, too. It was the one thing I had going for me, but watching her sing, watching her put on a show for the audience and sing for me, to me, was indescribable.

The adrenaline rush was keeping me awake thinking about her and this little game we were playing, because that was what this was, right? A game. We were tricking the public, her fans, that's all this was. It was a game, and I'd be damned if it was a game I lost.

I heard a rustling noise and felt the Mount Everest of comfort start to move. I saw her hand graze its way under the pillows and feel around. When she found my hand, she squeezed it lightly. I just blinked at her hand in mine.

A breath later, I heard her ask, "Is this okay?"

Despite myself, I grinned and squeezed back, nodding. I couldn't deny it felt nice.

"My?" She pulled her hand back.

The old nickname did me in. I was glad for the pillow wall hiding how wide I was grinning until a second later it came toppling down on me with force and knocked the breath out of me. Hollywood shoved the pillows off us, leaving her body on top of mine. She was watching me, and I couldn't help but laugh.

Her look of concern melted when she heard that, and was swiftly replaced with confusion. "What?"

I was too busy laughing to respond.

"What?" she asked again, louder. She started shaking my shoulders lightly. "What is it?"

I was still laughing. She grew more insistent. "Come on, tell me!"

"Only you would ask if it's okay to hold my hand and then leap on top of me," I said through laughter.

She blinked, surprised, looking down at me and seeming to realize for the first time just how close we were. "I can move if-" she started, but I stopped her.

"It's okay, you're fine. I mean, you had your tongue down my throat. We probably don't need the pillow wall anymore," I said, laughing.

At that, she grinned and batted her eyelashes at me and said, "You liked it."

I would let myself be dragged to hell before admitting it, but she was right, I loved it.

"I'm not the one throwing myself at you."

She pulled away, and I already missed her body against mine.

For once, I let myself speak without thinking. "Tell you what," I said tentatively. "How about we get rid of the wall? I could use a cuddle buddy."

At that, she looked at me in surprise before grinning. "Really?"

I nodded, and we both started moving the pillows out of the way, tossing them onto the floor, which took much longer than I expected. "Geez, Sav, could you have any more pillows?"

It wasn't until she stopped moving that I realized my faux pas. I hadn't called her Sav in a long time, since the show ended. I had lost myself for a minute there, had forgotten to be mad at her, forgotten to have my guard up. I pointedly added, "Shouldn't surprise me from a diva like you, though, Hollywood."

The conflicting emotions that rushed over her face almost made me feel bad. Almost. As I watched, she quickly blinked them away and we finished moving the pillows.

I waited with interest to see what she would do, and was surprised when she still scooted closer and nuzzled her head into my chest, resting against my shoulder. Her honeysuckle shampoo was making me feel dizzy. I quickly looked away when she moved her head to look at me.

I felt her lips touch my cheek, and she softly said, "Thank you for having my back today."

She started to lay back down on my shoulder, but suddenly popped back up.

I looked at her and waited for her to say something, or do something. She had moved over to join me, but if I somehow crossed a line, I wasn't going to make things worse. After a moment, she reached out her hand, stopping it hovering over my shoulder, and asked, "Can I?"

I blinked at her, looked at her hand, and then back to her face. I had no clue what she was asking, but I was curious enough to find out that it didn't stop me from saying, "Yes."

She reached out and I was surprised when she started tracing the lines of my tattoo, "It's beautiful," she breathed out.

A tentative smile formed on my lips. I loved my tattoo. I had taken a lot of time thinking about it and finding just the right design. It was a black ornate hourglass with sand slipping down, surrounded by black and white sunflowers. I loved how perfect it was. I had gotten it to remind myself how short life is. The hourglass with the slipping sand showed how futile it is to try to slow down life. No matter what you do, time is going to pass, but you get to decide how you spend it.

The sunflowers were my sister's favorite, probably because our Gram told us they were our mother's favorite. Neither of us were old enough to concrete memories of our mother, but the sunflowers helped me feel a little closer to her and to my sister. Sunflowers also represented peace and positivity, the perfect contrast and balance to the hourglass's inevitably of death.

I waited for her to ask what it meant like everyone did, but instead she said, "I'm sure you mother would have loved it."

I lay there speechless, feeling my eyes water. It was crazy being so seen by someone that I didn't have to say a word. She continued to trace the lines and I felt like I had to say something, so I said the first thing I could think to. "Am I that easy to read?"

She shrugged and met my eye, "I don't know if I'd say you are in general, but I'd like to think I still know some things about you."

The openness in her expression had me speaking without thinking. "You do. You only missed the crappier parts of my life. The tattoo used to be just for my mother, now it's a reminder that Gram's getting worse and there's nothing I can do for her besides be there for her." My voice broke and I felt tears start to form, but the words didn't stop. "I'm doing this for her, we needed the money, but no amount of money in the world can stop time. Even with the best doctors, medicines, and treatments, she doesn't have much longer."

I was crying now fully and felt Sav snuggle into me, putting her arms around me. "Gram's sick?" she asked, her voice wavering as much as my own had.

"She's okay right now. Elite hooked her up with a nurse and private chef and they let me talk to her every day, but I feel so damn guilty for being here. I'm doing this for her, but I feel so guilty about no being with her."

"I'm so sorry. I had no idea she was sick. If there's anything at all I can do, promise me you'll let me know."

I hated accepting charity more than anything, but for Gram's sake, I could push down my pride. "She's okay for now, but if things get worse and she needs something, I promise I'll let you know."

"Thank you," she said softly. "I miss her, you know. Her and little Leslie. How's Leslie doing anyway?"

I chuckled a little at that, knowing Leslie would hate being called little, "She's not so little anymore. Her divorce finalized last year, so she's doing so much better."

I felt her breath catch at that and almost felt bad bringing it up.

"How was it for her?" she asked quietly.

I wasn't sure what she was looking for, so I opted for the truth. "As good as these things can go, it got a little messy with Kat for a bit there, but she got primary custody thankfully."

I felt her head tilt when she asked, "Who's Kat?"

I felt a little rush of guilt and sadness that she didn't even know about Kat, especially at the thought of how much Kat would love her. Sav looked like a grown-up Barbie and Kat would be obsessed with her.

"Little Leslie has a little girl. I'm an Auntie." I said grinning.

"Shut up! No way!"

"Yes way!"

"The millisecond we get our phones back you're showing me five million pictures. In fact, I'm mad at you that I haven't seen any yet." Her enthusiasm was endearing.

"Auntie Maya," she muses. "I can see it. You're definitely the coolest, queerest aunt around. I bet she loves your purple hair."

I laughed, "of course she does. It's unicorn hair." I said still laughing.

She burst into laughter at that. "I never thought I would hear the day that you proudly proclaimed you have unicorn hair."

"What can I say? I'm gorgeous and my hair is niece-approved."

"You're right. Definitely gorgeous."

I felt my heart speed up at that, and tried to calm down before she noticed, "me or my hair?"

"Both, obviously," she said easily. "I missed your gorgeous face, My." I didn't know what to say to that, so I ran my fingers through her hair. "I hate that I've missed so much. I really hope that after all this we can stay in touch."

I sucked in a breath, not knowing what I thought or what to say.

She filled the silence before I could, "I'm not asking you to make any decision now, I'm just asking you to think about it and making my opinion clear. Clarice told us how important communication is, so this is me communicating."

I laughed at that and wanted to make a joke, but she was being so open, that I felt she deserved some honesty too. "Being here is turning out to not be the worst thing."

I felt her smile as she said, "That'll be my new tagline: Savannah Hollywood, not the worst. That would make a great t-shirt" We both chuckled at that before she added, "but I'm really glad to have you here. For what it's worth, I wouldn't want to do this with anyone else, and I'm sorry I hurt you."

With that knocking me speechless, she settled in. After a few minutes, her breathing evened out as she fell into sleep. I was left there staring at the ceiling, smelling her honeysuckle shampoo. There was no way I was going to be able to turn my mind off tonight.

FROM ICON TO BI-CON:
THE SAVANNAH HOLLYWOOD COMING OUT STORY

Savannah Hollywood, America's sweetheart and popstar royalty just came out of the closet, taking the world by surprise when she announced she's bisexual. With those few words, she transformed from icon to bi-con. She told the world that she didn't want to stay hidden anymore, and we commend her bravery. Before any young ladies out there get any ideas, we need to add that she also introduced the world to her new girlfriend, Maya Ryder. If the name sounds familiar, it's because you've likely seen her and Hollywood's names linked in the past. Maya Ryder was Savannah's old costar from her days acting in Hollywood High.

On the show they played rivals but inside sources say that in real life that couldn't have been further from the truth. Behind the scenes, they were thick as thieves. Is it possible love was blooming way back then? They had a falling out after the show ended, but it seems like this romance is getting its second chance, and who doesn't love a good second chance romance? One thing's for sure, we'll be streaming Hollywood High this weekend watching to see where it all began.

AND THE FANS GO WILD...

Just when we thought it was impossible for Savannah to get any more popular, she endeared herself to a new group of fans by coming out as bisexual. People have been printing her face on shirts superimposed over the bisexual flag and the rainbow flag. We interviewed some of her fans to see what they thought of their idol's latest admission.

"I used to like Savannah, and now I love her. I can't believe how brave she is and I'm so proud of her for living her truth." – Lily, 25

"I never used to listen to Savannah's music. Nothing personal, I just normally avoid the more mainstream stuff, especially pop, but seeing her take a stand for me and my people won me over. She's got herself a new fan." - Jayson, 34

"I can't believe my OTP is playing out in real life! I have written so much fanfiction about Savannah and Maya's characters from Hollywood High, I can't believe I'm getting to watch it play out in real life. To all my haters who said they had no chemistry in Hollywood High, you can suck it! I was right!" – Hannah, 23

"I loved her before and I love her just as much now. It doesn't change anything for me, and why should it? I just hope that whoever she ends up with, she's happy." – Jennifer, 27

"I have been so afraid to live my own truth, seeing Savannah unapologetically live her truth and date whoever she wants gave me the courage to come out too. If it wasn't for her, I would still be hiding in the closet. She gave me the courage, and I'm sure I'm not the only one. Savannah, if you ever see this, on behalf of all the queers out there, thank you for giving us hope, someone to look up to, and a renewed sense of pride in being part of such a wonderful community." – Sadie, 30

Well, there you have it, we wouldn't have said it better ourselves. Gay, straight, bi or whatever she wants to be, the world loves Savannah Hollywood and there's no changing that.

CHAPTER 21

MAYA

I had been reading over her shoulder, my hand braced on her shoulder, when she lowered the magazine. I was startled to see water staining the page. I moved to her side and saw that she was crying. I cupped her chin with my hand, examining her carefully. It was a lot, definitely an emotional day, but I was worried about her.

I was surprised to notice that the worry didn't feel like betraying my own feelings like it had before. She needed me, well she needed someone and I was there. As her live in lesbian I was as good as anyone for the job. No matter how weird things were between us, I would never let a fellow queer down in their time of need. If she needed cheering up, I would be her cheerleader. *Actually, that sounds too straight, I'll be her queerleader.* I almost chuckled at the thought before quickly turning my attention back to her. "They-" she started before stopping again. I couldn't tell what she was feeling and not knowing was worrying me, but I knew I needed to wait for her to speak.

"They love me." The wonder in her voice struck me with surprise.

"Of course they do. You're Savannah freaking Hollywood. The world loves you."

She smiled a little at that and said, "They loved the America's sweetheart straight girl they thought I was. I wasn't sure what they would think about the truth."

I blinked at the earnestness in her expression. She really had thought they might not like her. That was shocking to me, and endeared her to me a little more. It was easier to see her as the same old Sav she used to be, my Sav, when she was vulnerable like this. It was getting harder and harder to keep Savannah Hollywood and my Sav separate in my mind. To distract myself and stop my thoughts from spiraling, I asked, "And what's the truth?"

She chuckled a little at gesturing to herself, "You should know better than anyone. The truth is I'm just me. I'm not the 'great Savannah Hollywood', I'm not the great anything, I'm just me, just Savannah. I try to be honest and kind, I care too much about a lot of things and people, and my life is a little messy. I'm a true chaos bi and I'm learning to be okay with that."

I laughed at that, relieved to see her smiling back at me. "I'm so proud of you," I told her.

"Thank you. You being here, going through this with me means the world to me. I know you're not really here by choice," she said, her smile dipping a moment and my traitorous heart flipped at it before she recovered a somewhat dimmer smile, "but I couldn't do this with anyone else at my side. You're my day one and I wouldn't have been half as brave without you."

"I'm not brave," I said quickly, not able to wrap my head around the rest of what she said. Running away from her words and any unwanted truths I might find in them. I wasn't brave, not really. "Not as brave as you," I admitted, so quietly that she had leaned in closer to hear me. It was the truth though. I wasn't nearly as brave as she was, or honest, or caring as her. Although no one could be as caring as her, she cared a lot about a lot.

"If I'm brave, it's because of you."

With that, she did the last thing I expected and closed the distance between us taking my lips in hers. She kissed me softly, caressing my lips with hers. Tentative, hopeful, and I answered her with kisses of my own. My body and heart already knew what my brain was trying to ignore, I was trapped. Not by contract, but by my own stupid heart. Savannah had never given back the piece of my heart I had given her when we were younger and now, she was back to claim the rest. For better or worse, she had more of my heart than anyone ever had.

Her kiss tasted salty and I chuckled against her lips. She pulled back, grinning before moving her face into an exaggerated pout, "What's so funny?"

"Your kisses taste like the ocean."

That startled a laugh out of her at the sound I couldn't help laughing too.

We were interrupted by the ringing of her phone. She gave me an apologetic smile before looking to see who it was. "It's Lexi," she said, watching me, "probably about the tabloids, but I should take it." She still hadn't answered though. I realized with a start, she was waiting for me to tell her it was okay.

"Of course, don't worry about it!" I said quickly. I didn't understand why she was so worried, but she seemed to calm a little and at that with one more look at me to be sure, she answered the phone. She pushed her chair back from the table and excused herself, but before she left, I could hear Lexi squealing on the phone. I smiled at Savannah's retreating form, happy she had more than just me to celebrate with. Which quickly reminded me how she had celebrated. Savannah Hollywood had *kissed* me. She had kissed *me*. Not in public, not to prove anything, just because she wanted to.

She had wanted to kiss me, and she might want to do it again. That brought a grin to my lips and thrill to my heart. I could kiss Savannah Hollywood whenever I wanted. No, I corrected myself, I could kiss Sav whenever I wanted. She might be Savannah Hollywood to the world, but to me she was just Sav, my Sav. My brilliant, beautiful, chaotic, bighearted Sav.

I couldn't wait for her to get off the phone again so I could show her how happy I was to be here.

CHAPTER 22

MAYA

When Sav had come bursting back into the room after getting off the phone with Lexi, shouting, "I'm playing Pride! I'm freaking headlining Pride!" I had rushed to her and pulled her into my arms, celebrating with her, radiating pride as I swallowed my own jealousy. I was trying to be better, not to be as bitter about her success. After all, she was a singer, my passion was acting. If she had been an actress, I might not have been able to curb my jealousy, but as it was, I found myself slowly able to be happy for her.

I had been to Pride before, of course. It wasn't my first parade, but nothing had prepared me for the pure energy we were hit with when we stepped out of the limo. Where Sav had found a rainbow limo on this short of notice during the biggest Pride event in the state, I had no idea, but between Lexi and Clarice with Elite's backing, it didn't surprise me. Those two alone could move mountains by sheer force of will.

The flashes and screams greeted us as we exited onto a rainbow carpet lined with security every couple of feet and a velvet rope keeping people out, but just barely. They were screaming, and it wasn't just Savannah's name I was hearing.

My heart swelled hearing a lot of people saying my name, that they loved me. It was intoxicating. Not just that people loved me, but the diversity of the crowd. Genders and sexualities all over the spectrum greeted me in faces as diverse as Los Angeles was. I was hit with an overwhelming amount of gratitude at being here, at getting to live in this time as an out and proud lesbian woman, able to show my love for a woman in public. A right that had been hard fought for and was still being fought for, but progress was staring me in the face and it was hard to feel anything but gratitude and pride. Proud of myself for being myself, of Savannah for living her truth, and of the many many people that had gathered here today to celebrate queer love however it looks.

Sav looked at me and grinned. That grin told me that she felt what I did. I felt her understanding and wonder and couldn't hold myself back. I didn't need to and heavens knew I didn't want to. I laced my arm around her back and spun her to me, kissing her beautiful smile. The screams got louder as she kissed me back. Her lips moved against mine with passion, passion that was going to get us both in trouble. I pulled away, leaving her and myself a little breathless. The crowd was loving it.

I looked to her again and she took my hand. I was happy to follow her lead. Today was her day; she had earned it. I was surprised when instead of heading down the carpet she moved toward the rope holding back the fans. I dropped my hand from hers in my surprise when she stepped within reach and posed for a picture with one of the fans. A moment later she turned her head to her right and then left before turning back around, spotting me, and she waved me over.

I moved to her, heat flushing my cheeks as I leaned to her ear and whispered, "Are you sure?"

I was happy just to be here, to be witnessing this triumph of hers. I didn't need to share in the spotlight.

"Absolutely. It wouldn't be a true Pride celebration without my girl at my side."

I grinned at that, knowing it was for show, but not hating the sound of being hers. I had it bad and I could only hope she treated my heart better than she had when we were younger.

CHAPTER 23

SAVANNAH

Walking the rainbow carpet with Maya had been the best I had felt in a long time. Seeing so many people had come out to support me was incredible, but seeing so many queer people here cheering for me was a different experience altogether. Even backstage now I could hear how loudly they were cheering and couldn't wait to go on and give them some of the same energy they were giving.

I grinned at the latest round of cheers and peeked around the corner to see Miss Lucy Fur dropping it low to a sped-up version of Sam Smith's Unholy. Miss Lucy knew how to work an outfit and a crowd. She had, of course, handpicked my outfit for tonight. I was decked out in the bisexual flag colors and glitter. My bodysuit was a blend of purple and blue and I was wearing bright pink bedazzled tights with silver glitter booties. I had given Miss Lucy free reign and she had gotten me a bi flag cape. I felt like a gay superhero and I loved everything minute of it. It was perfect.

Miss Lucy had told me that if she was going to be anyone's opening act, they had to be as well dressed as she was. I was going to miss her when Elite's job was over. Her and Clarice, too, who was quickly endearing herself to me."

My eyes searched backstage for the other person I was thinking of as I tried not to think about her being on the list of people I was going to miss when this was all over. I felt like I was just getting her back, and losing her again was the last thing I wanted to think about. I didn't see her. The last I saw her she was talking to Stevie and Nikki before I was ushered to my cue backstage. Stevie, Nikki, and Connor would be waiting on the other side for our cues. I had hoped Maya would come find me, but so far, no luck.

I heard the last notes of Unholy and knew from the wild cheers that whatever Miss Lucy was doing, they were loving it.

A few moments later, to deafening cheers, she made her way off the stage and over to me. Her outfit was sinfully red. Her bright red leotard was paired with thigh high red leather boots and her signature flamed cape. She even had horns sticking out of her voluminous red wig.

I wrapped her in a hug and squealed, "You were amazing!"

She grinned. "Don't I know it, darling. You're going to slay out there."

I paled a little at that. "To be honest, I'm a little nervous. I don't get why, though. I've done a lot of shows like this."

"Honey," she said, looking at me with disbelief, "you've done a lot of big shows, but you've never done a queer show."

She was right, of course. This was a big first for me and would definitely be a show I remembered forever. It was crazy to think that I was out of the closet, free to be myself, and there was a giant crowd out there loving me the more for it.

Miss Lucy gripped my shoulders and said, "Deep breath and then get your beautiful ass out there. They'll love you."

I smiled and wrapped my arms around her waist, hugging her tightly before letting her go.

"Go on, honey. You've shed your cocoon and became a beautiful gay butterfly and I'm so proud of you. Savannah Hollywood, from icon to bi-con."

I was starting to tear up, and she tutted at me, "The makeup! Think of the makeup!"

I chuckled at that and took another deep breath. "Go kill it, darling." With a swat on my butt, she sent me toward the stage with a last parting, "You're bi-conic!"

I was still grinning when I stepped onstage and the roar of the crowd greeted me. I let it wash over me, basking in it as I squinted out past the stage lights looking at the crowd. My heart soared at all the pride flags and proud queers I saw there cheering for me. I looked back and saw Connor's goofy grin, Stevie's triumphant smile, and Nikki's wide-eyed wonder. I loved them all but they weren't who I wanted to see. I looked to the other side of the stage and locked eyes with Maya. She smiled broadly and I was struck by the pride in her eyes as she took in the crowd cheering for me.

I was enjoying every moment of it, but couldn't help feeling like I didn't deserve it, that others deserved to be here performing at Pride more than I did. A particular someone specifically. I might not be able to change the past, but right here, right now, I had some power.

As I crossed to the microphone, I weighed my options. Elite should be okay with the deviation from the plan, but I was pretty sure my record label wouldn't like it. I was pretty sure they wouldn't like me being openly queer at all, but they'd been mercifully quiet about it so far. I knew my luck wouldn't last. They were going to call me in eventually and it was going to be bad, but I couldn't bring myself to care. Why not give them one more thing to be mad about? Feeling my plans change with each step as I approached the mic.

"Thank you all so much. Your love and support means the world to me. I'm so proud to be out here with you all and so honored to be performing for you all."

I waited for the cheers to die down enough before saying, "I can't wait to sing for you all, but I'm not the only one."

I plucked the microphone from the stand and was already on the move. Maya's eyes widened at me, and she looked behind her. I couldn't believe she actually looked behind her, like I had eyes for anyone but her. "I have a very special guest here with me tonight. I'm going to grab them but why don't you give them a warm welcome." Before the words left my mouth, they were already screaming again. I ducked backstage and took Maya's hand in mine, holding the microphone away from me, and asked, "Sing with me?"

"But it's your night," she protested.

"Sing with me," I repeated, no longer a question now a plea.

"But I don't know your songs."

"You'll know this one," I said with a grin, pulling her toward me. She held fast for a moment before relenting and letting me lead her out onstage. The stage hands were damn good at their jobs and had a second microphone waiting in the wings. Nikki was already moving to grab it for us. When she brought it to me, I grinned and mouthed, "thank you". I wanted to thank her properly but I was sure she wouldn't hear me over the roar of the crowd. I still hoped she would see the gratitude in my eyes. They hadn't actually spent any time with Maya yet, so it meant the world to me they were supporting me in this.

Maya was looking out at the crowd in shock, her eyes watering, and I would have given up a thousand spotlights to see that look on her face.

I turned the crowd and asked, "Are you ready for a Hollywood High throwback?"

The crowd cheered and Maya's eyes flew to mine at the opening notes. She knew this song. Of course she did. It was her favorite performance song of ours from the show. The song was a battle of dominance between us as we both fought for the spotlight. It was catchy, powerful, and fun to perform and the fire in her eyes told me I was going to have to bring my A-game. Things might be getting better between us, but she was going to give this everything.

"You better sing your heart out, Hollywood."

The crowd screamed, and I couldn't help myself from saying, "You're on, Ryder."

Maya's first words drowned out the crowd's response, but my eyes were only for her.

It wasn't until the song was over and I was hot and flushed that I realized how much sexual tension was built into the song, into the rivalry in it. No wonder people had shipped our characters so hard. I couldn't wait to fall into bed with her tonight and see if we could make that passion come together off stage, too.

CHAPTER 24

MAYA

Singing at the LA Pride Festival had been a dream I didn't even know I had. It was exhilarating and pure bliss. More than that, singing with Sav, her wanting to share the moment with me, was incredible. It wasn't just any performance, it was Pride, it was for our people. I was still awestruck she had shared the spotlight and the victory with me. I was still riding the high of the performance when we collapsed into bed.

I should have been tired. It had been a long day for us both, but I was still buzzed on adrenaline and couldn't think of anything besides Sav laying next to me in a little silk nightie that I wanted to rip off of her. She was so damn gorgeous. She sighed contentedly as she settled into her pillow and I knew I should let her sleep, but I wanted every inch of her she was willing to give.

"Come here," I said in a low, commanding voice. She turned to me, her eyes wide, but didn't move.

"Closer," I said and she moved, closing the foot of distance between us. She moved closer until her face was inches from mine, her chest pressed against my shoulder. I could feel her nipples peaked through the silk fabric and knew she wanted this almost as badly as I did.

"Like this?" she asked not moving any closer.

"Closer," I said lacing my fingers through her hair and pressing her lips to mine. I was starving for her, but her need and passion surprised me. Her tongue pressed inside my mouth and I groaned in surprise. Her hands moved to my hair as she pulled me closer. I let my free roam to her chest and brushed over her peaked nipples through the silk fabric. I felt her shiver under my touch and I moved my hand lower. I caressed her hip and around to her ass. I squeezed her through the fabric and she moaned into my mouth. I paused a moment, waiting to see if she wanted me to keep going. She whined and pressed herself harder to me, pressing her chest against mine. I moaned at the feel of her and dipped my hand below the fabric, feeling the curve of her ass, the warmth of her skin, no fabric. She wasn't wearing anything under her slip of a dress.

She shivered against my touch pressing herself to me harder. I pulled away from her lips and heard her whimper. "What's wrong, baby?"

She pressed into me trying to pull my lips back to hers but I didn't let her move me closer.

She groaned, "I need you. Touch me." She was half pleading, half demanding. I so badly wanted to touch her, but she wasn't the one in charge.

"How about a please?" I asked, letting my fingers skim over her nipple.

"Please," she gasped. "I need to be touched."

I could work with that.

"So do it,"

Her eyes moved to mine and widened, "Do what?"

"Show me how you like to be touched."

She didn't have to be told twice. I pulled further away, watching as she pulled up her dress. She parted her legs and dipped a finger into her folds. It came out glistening. She moved up and started working slow circles around her clit. Watching her undid me. I needed a closer view. I moved down her body licked at her nipple through the silk while flicking the other. I felt her shudder and with satisfaction moved lower, over her stomach down to where her hand was working her. She gasped out as I blew air over her clit. She went to move her hand, but I quickly blocked her with my own hand.

"Keep going. Show me what you like."

She whimpered but did as she was told. I kept my hand over hers, feeling her work herself. I slipped lower and pressed my lips against her inner thigh alternating kisses and gentle nibbles. Every time my teeth grazed her thigh, she moaned. The third time, I couldn't take it anymore and slipped my hand under the waistband of my shorts, dipping into my underwear and started working my clit the same way she was to hers. With my hand still over hers, I felt her movements and mirrored them on myself.

When I started to moan, I moved up to watch her for a moment. Seeing her coming undone was so damn hot. I licked up her folds, stopping right before her clit where our hands were. I licked back down and dipped my tongue inside her, tasting her. Her desire tasted so sweet coating my tongue. She whimpered at the contact and ground her hips against me as I moved my tongue in and out of her. Her fingers quickened matching my movements and my own did the same quickly bringing the both of us to the edge.

With one last thrust of my tongue and her soft cry, I felt her come undone, pushing me over the edge. I lapped up her sweetness as I shuddered through my own release.

When her fingers stopped moving, I gave her one last taste before moving away. I went to wipe my face with my tank top, but she stopped me, "Come here," she whispered.

I moved to her and she pressed her lips to mine. Her tongue moved against my lips, so I let her in. We kissed slowly, lazily, sharing in her taste. A few moments later, I pulled away and pulled her back to me, cuddling her body against me.

She started to protest, but I pulled her tighter and planted a kiss on the top of her head, "It's been a long day. You need your sleep."

She grumbled, but she was already relaxing in my arms. We both had a long day, and the only thing I wanted now was to fall asleep with her in my arms. It wasn't long before sleep took us both.

CHAPTER 25

SAVANNAH

The call I was dreading came the day after the performance, waking me and Maya in a cold dose of reality. I hadn't warned her about my record label, not really. I hadn't thought she would care before, and now, I wasn't sure what we were but I was sure she cared in some way, and now I was just ashamed. I hated the way that they treated me, hated how stupid I had been.

When I had signed my life away to the Hollywood High producers, I had done so without a second thought, without anyone having my best interest at heart, I was alone and naive. I loved the show with everything in me. I had wanted to move on to a singing career, but when it came time to leave, I hated that they were able to force my hand, that I didn't have a say in how I left or the timing. It was made even worse by the fact that the man who held my future in his hands was Bronson, the slimeball who ruined things between me and Maya. He took my best friend from me.

By the time the contract finally expired, things had changed for me. I had much more negotiating power. I was a pretty well-known singer, not anywhere near as famous as I was now, but things were different for me. I wasn't alone anymore. I had Darren. I loved him with everything in me and trusted him with my life, so when he told me I should join his friend's record label, I jumped at the opportunity. I was sick of being used and pushed around and couldn't believe my luck that I would have control back. I trusted Darren and trusted those he trusted. Like our prenup, I didn't bother hiring a lawyer to look over the papers, just signed them on his word.

Now, I was embarrassed how naïve I was. I wondered if he ever loved me or if he just loved how much I worshiped him. Our relationship was a fairytale until my popularity started eclipsing his. All of a sudden it wasn't famous actor Darren Dawson and his wife, singer Savannah Hollywood, it was popstar icon Savannah Hollywood and her husband, actor Darren Dawson. He had hated it. I could see clearly now how thinly veiled his contempt and jealousy were but I hadn't noticed them then.

Since him and I had split, things with my record label, Hedge Fund Records, had become more hostile. My contract was coming to a close, though. I only owed them one more album before I was free. They should have been playing nice, trying to win my favor so I might re-sign with them, but they weren't. It chilled me that they weren't courting me. It made me feel like I had all those years ago sitting at the boardroom table with Bronson and the other studio execs, like I was outmatched and out of my depths.

I hoped that all the meeting was about was them being angry about my sexuality. I hadn't consulted them on making an announcement. I wasn't sure any of them had even know. I hadn't even told Darren. At the time, I would have sworn it was because I loved him so much that it didn't matter. He was my one and only. Now, I wondered if I had worried he might not have accepted me. He was cruel and judgmental when things weren't just the way he wanted them and I wasn't sure if my sexuality would have fit his image.

The thought pissed me off and I held tightly to the anger as I rushed through getting ready, wanting to get this over with.

CHAPTER 26

MAYA

Sav was more shaken than I think I had ever seen her. She wouldn't tell me anything and we had quickly gotten ready without more than a few words exchanged. She was shutting me out. Sav wasn't like that though, she didn't handle things the way I did. She didn't shut down, she didn't rage, she cried. She was an emotional person through and through and to see her beyond tears, beyond emotion, was terrifying.

She had even tried to leave me at home. I told her she wasn't going without me. I saw panic flash in her eyes a moment before it bowed to acceptance. That easy acceptance underscored just how wrong things were. She was passionate and I was worried seeing her so cowed. She walked to our ride like a woman walking to her death, like she had no energy left to fear the inevitable. It lit a fire in me and made me wonder for the first time if maybe Sav's cushy life wasn't everything I thought.

Before we got in the car, she made me promise that whatever they said or did in there, I wouldn't say anything to them, wouldn't argue with them. The seriousness on her face had me agreeing and then left me worrying the entire way there about what the hell we were walking into and if I had made a promise I couldn't keep.

The boardroom we were left waiting in was as cold and unwelcoming as the rest of the studio building. The large table cramped the space and the chairs were clearly chosen for discomfort, not wanting their occupants to linger. It didn't escape my notice that the chairs on the other side of the table looked noticeably more comfortable. The air conditioning was on full blast, chilling me to my bones, but one look at Sav's goosebumps had me grumbling and begrudgingly taking off my jacket. I looped it around her shoulders and she jumped in surprise, startled from her thoughts and smiled weakly at me before drawing it tightly around herself.

I forced a smile too, and leaned her into me. "Remind me again why Lexi isn't here?" I asked in a hushed tone. The room making me feel like we were being watched, like we were in enemy territory. I wasn't Lexi's biggest fan, but it seemed like this was an important meeting and it was odd to me Sav hadn't brought her legal counsel.

"Because it's just a strategy meeting for my new album," I could tell she was trying hard to convince both her and myself of this. I hoped she at least convinced herself, because I wasn't convinced. "It would look bad if I brought a lawyer."

I didn't think it mattered how she looked when she was this worried. She needed someone else on her side and I wished Lexi was here, hell even Clarice. Someone else besides me to stand up for her too.

I was stopped from saying so when the door whooshed open, bringing an unwelcome rush of cold air and a group of suits with calculating smiles. The one with the most expensive looking haircut seated himself directly across from Sav with a wide grin. "Sav-an-nah" he dragged out, "It's been ages. How are you sweetheart?"

I watched her swallow tightly before putting on a false smile, "Well thank you. I think this album might have the best sales yet," she said with a forced cheerfulness.

"I can't say I agree," he said matter of factly, and I watched her pale.

"You don't like it?" she asked.

"The album is neither here nor there. The focus groups liked it well enough."

"That's great!" she said, relieved, but from the record exec's expression, I knew she spoke too soon.

"What I can't say I agree with is your behavior lately."

"I'm not sure I understand you. I've been promoting the album and doing the press circuits like you wanted."

"Like I wanted?" he asked quietly. "You think this is what I wanted?"

I paled at the tone in his voice, and reached under the table for Sav's hand. I felt her hand shaking when I took it in mine and gave it a light squeeze.

"I think you wanted me to make headlines."

"I wanted you to continue making hits. I didn't want you alienating half your fan base with your latest whim. I wanted the press focused on your divorce, not your latest hookup."

I was biting my tongue so hard I could swear I tasted blood. What a homophobic, bigoted trashcan of a man.

"Alienating my fan base?" Sav asked. I couldn't tell if she was playing dumb or just hoping she misunderstood him.

"Your younger fans might be okay with that liberal gay agenda shit you're pedaling, but you had no right to do that without consulting us."

I was seeing red, and was about to burst when I felt Sav squeeze my hand back, I looked to her and saw a little bit of the woman I knew had returned, a little of her fire. I took a breath and tried to squelch mine.

"I'm sure I must be misunderstanding, Mark. All I did was tell the world something new about me. I'm bisexual. It's a fact, not a political stance."

Mark took a breath and announced, "Clear the room." No one moved. "Now!" he yelled with a snap of his fingers and the other suits jumped out of their seats. I wasn't sure what to do, but Sav's small shake of her head had me staying put.

He looked at her and then at me, eyebrows raised in challenge neither of us moved. He let out another breath as the door closed.

"Fine, she can stay. I don't care, and I don't care if your little stunt was a fact or a stance, Hedge Fund Records owns you. You're our property and you don't so much as breath without our say so."

"You wouldn't have wanted me to come out?"

"We wouldn't have let you," he said with a snarl, "But now you've backed us into an impossible position that we'll have to maneuver you out of."

She squeezed my hand, "What would you like me to do?"

"We've decided it would be best for everyone if this little charade ends. Break up with your *girlfriend*," he said with a sneer, "and go crawling back to Darren like a good little wife."

I was clenching my free hand tight enough that my nails were digging into my palm. I had no idea how she was staying so calm and I was livid at hearing her treated this way.

I couldn't stop myself from wondering how long they had been treating her like this, how long she had been putting up with this and if she really thought it was worth it. I shied away from the other thought that she had been alone in this. If she hadn't let ambition cloud her judgment, I might have been here to help her navigate it. We could have navigated it together. Instead, she had left me behind.

A few short weeks ago I would have been thrilled to know her fame wasn't all it was cracked up to be, but seeing how she was treated, especially now with how much I cared about her, I hated it. It was eating away at me not saying anything. I looked over at her, and saw there was a spark in her eye that hadn't been there before and that gave me the courage to remain silent. I wasn't sure I trusted her completely, but she had only asked one thing of me and I was going to do my best to keep my promise.

"I'm not his wife," she insisted, and then corrected, "or I won't be much longer, and who I date shouldn't be of concern to you or the rest of the label."

"I can't sell this album with a raging lesbian as the singer. But rest assured, the amount of records we'll sell when you stop being stubborn and go back to where you belong with your husband will make up for any inconvenience you've caused. You need him and his publicity to keep selling like you do. At his side, you'll make millions."

What the hell was wrong with this guy. She was way more popular than Darren Dawson was. If anything, he needed her, too bad he didn't get to have her.

"I think you misunderstand me. I have no interest in going back to my husband, nor is it your place to suggest it. Who I date is none of your concern, and most importantly, I'm bisexual, not a lesbian."

I squeezed her hand again, so incredibly proud of her.

"You're not anything but fooling yourself. I get it. Darren was running around on you so you wanted to find a way to hurt him. This was creative I'll give you that, but you can drop the act. He'll take you back."

"My sexuality isn't an act," she said slowly, enunciated each word so no mistake could be made.

"Isn't it? How'd you meet your new girl anyway?"

She paled a little at that but said, "I can hardly see how that matters."

"It mattered quite a lot to us, and to your husband, and I'm sure it would matter even more to your fans. It would be a shame if they found out."

I couldn't believe it. First the amount of disrespect and now her record label, who was supposed to be on her side, was flat out threatening her, because veiled or not, it was a threat. I knew as well as she did, if they came out and told everyone she had hired me to fake date her, no one would believe her sexuality and she would lose the respect of her fans. I couldn't let that happen to her, but I had no idea what to do for her. I was starting to think she was right, that maybe I should have sat out the meeting. I felt so useless.

She was white as a ghost but still managed to bite out, "What do you want, Mark?"

He broke out into a triumphant grin, "I thought you'd never ask," he said as he slid a stack of papers to her. I saw from the top it was a contract.

"What is it?" she asked.

"Your latest contract. Once you sign this, you'll have secured your spot with us for another five albums. Exciting, isn't it?"

"I'm not signing that."

"Ah ah ah, don't be so hasty Miss Hollywood. We made you and don't think for a second we couldn't take that away, and then where will you be? A sad lonely, divorced thirty year old without love, children, or a hope for a bright future, alone with your little lesbian girlfriend or whoever else you'll be desperate enough to sleep with for attention."

I shot out of my chair like lightening only to be pushed back into my chair by her hand on my shoulder as she pushed herself to standing. Her quick look at me told me she'd handle it and it sent a rush of heat through me.

"You'll watch how you speak about my girlfriend."

He laughed, actually laughed. "So quick to defend her, I would almost believe your little ruse. You're a better actress than I gave you credit for. I'm sure we can find a way to use that."

"I'm not signing anything."

"I would think long and hard about that, but not too long. You'll find I won't be feeling generous for long. The longer you wait the less favorable our terms, so actually do take as long as you'd like," he said with a grin, as he gestured to the door. "You can see yourselves out."

Sav squeezed my hand and I jumped up and let her lead me out of the room, happy to be out of there.

We almost ran through the halls in our haste to be out of the place. The moment we were back in the car, she started crying. I pulled her tight to me and held her as she cried. I had so much to say, but clearly it was going to have to wait.

CHAPTER 27

MAYA

It wasn't until she had showered and climbed into bed that she finally said, "I'm sure you have questions."

"What the hell was that?" I asked.

"It wasn't supposed to go that badly. I had a plan, but I didn't think Mark would have the audacity to actually threaten me."

"Why are you working with someone like that anyway?"

She sighed, "He's a friend of Darren's."

"Of course he is," I said, my eyes narrowing at the mention of him, but I tried to shake the anger, she needed me. "So, what was your plan?" I asked, hoping to distract her and myself.

She pulled out her phone and shuffled through her menu screens, clicking on an app that had a microphone icon. She scrolled to the top and hit play. Mark's voice came out of the speaker, a little muffled but undoubtably his as he said, "Sav-an-nah. It's been ages. How are you, sweetheart?"

It took me a moment to realize what it meant. She clicked it off with a shudder. I pulled her closer to me. She turned and I cradled her back to my chest, holding her tightly against me, before asking "Did you get all of it?"

"I did. I figured he would have some sort of homophobic shit to say that might end up helping me." She sighed before continuing, "That's why I asked you not to say anything. I didn't want either of us sounding bad on the recording. I didn't think he would threaten me though, not about something like this. It shouldn't surprise me though that he feels like if he can't have me, no one should."

"What are you saying?" I asked, thinking I understood, but not wanting to believe it.

"I don't think I have a choice. I'm probably going to have to sign the contract."

"You still want to work with him?"

"Of course not," she said quickly, frustration lacing her words, "but it doesn't sound like I have a choice."

"There has to be a choice. What about Lexi? There has to be something she can do?" I asked grasping for straws.

She shook her head sadly, "I signed the contract before I met her and it was a bad one. It sounds like this one could possibly be worse."

"So, what if he tells everyone about our arrangement? You really think they'll believe him?" I wanted to say more, to tell her how this didn't feel fake to me anymore, but I quieted myself.

"I don't know, and the uncertainty isn't worth the risk. He knows I won't risk it."

If I couldn't talk her out of this, maybe Lexi could, but only if Lexi knew in time to stop her.

"Promise me something," before she could agree or disagree, I rushed on, "Promise me you'll take a day to think about it. Just a day, promise me you won't sign tomorrow."

From the way she stiffened I knew she was thinking like I was about his threats about her waiting. I had no idea how much I was asking of her but I needed to try to get her out of this. Had the roles been reversed, she would have done it for me. I didn't know if a day would make a difference, but I needed to get Lexi to talk to her, and see if there was anything Lexi could do about the situation.

She nodded against me and I sagged in relief, "Okay. I can wait a day, but it won't change anything. I'm going to have to sign eventually."

As I held her tightly against me and felt her drift into sleep, I hoped with everything in me that she was wrong.

CHAPTER 28

MAYA

When Lexi answered the phone the next morning, I wasn't quite sure how to start, but decided to just go for it.

"Lexi, it's Maya. I need your help."

"If by you, you mean Savannah, then absolutely. If by you actually mean you, then it depends what you want."

I chuckled at that. Sav certainly had a type when it came to her friends, that's exactly the answer I would've given if I were in her shoes.

"Of course it's for Sav."

"I don't know why you would think that was obvious. You're not exactly her biggest fan."

I was a little taken aback by that, not sure what it meant that Lexi didn't seem to be up to speed on how things had progressed between me and Sav. I ignored it though, now wasn't the time for that. I wasn't entirely sure what it was that was going on between us anyway, I just knew I needed to help her and I needed Lexi's help to do it.

"Please," I asked again. "She needs our help and for some reason she's not keen on asking."

She took a breath, before replying, "What's going on?" I rushed to tell her about the meeting yesterday, glossing over some of the worse insults.

"Those bastards!" She snarled. "No wonder Savannah doesn't let me anywhere near them. I would have made her break the contract myself if I knew they were treating her like that."

Hope swelled in me at her words, "the contract can be broken?"

She sighed, "Easily? Probably not. It's been a while since I've combed over it. I know she could opt out with a monetary penalty if she stopped her music-"

"She can't!" I interrupted, shocked she would even mention it, "That would kill her."

"I know," she said sadly. "I'd like to say I can't believe they're doing this to her, but Hedge Fund Records is made up of a bunch of douchey trust fund frat bros, and they're all in Darren's pocket. Of course they're doing everything they can to make her miserable. She was just about to be free. Free of him, free of the label, and now here they are trying to leash her again."

"There has to be something we can do," I said pleading, whether it was with her or the universe I wasn't sure.

"I'm not sure. Tell you what I have a few meetings this morning and then I'll clear the rest of my day. I'll come over with three copies of the contract and some highlighters and see if three heads are better than one."

It was worth a shot and was more hope than I had before talking to her. I thanked her and ended the call. I was glad that Sav hadn't been alone dealing with this, but it was hurting me to think I had chosen to abandon her to all of this. At least I was here now, though and I would do everything I could to help.

Chapter 29

Savannah

The doorbell rang unexpectedly, I looked up from my notebook, the beginnings of song lyrics scrawled out, crossed out, and rewritten in front of me. It was supposed to be one of our few days off and I had no idea who that could be.

My eyes met Maya's and she looked a little guilty. "Are you expecting someone?" I asked.

She quickly jumped up and said, "I'll get it." I noticed she didn't answer my question, and she opened the door without looking through the peephole.

In swept a tornado of blonde hair wearing a look of grim determination and carrying a mountain of papers. I looked back and forth between Maya and Lexi. Maya looked sheepish, which was odd to see on her. She rarely ever looked unsure of anything. Lexi set the papers down on the table, reaching into her purse and threw something at me where I sat nestled in my reading chair. I saw a purple object flying at me and managed to catch it before it whacked me in the face.

I looked at it, a purple highlighter, and looked back at her questioningly. I didn't think it was possible to be more confused than I was.

"What are you doing here?" I asked, and held up the highlighter, "and why the highlighter?"

She shrugged and held up the green and pink ones, "did you want another color?"

I shook my head, "no purple is fine," I said carefully. I was about to re-ask my question when she spoke before I could.

"Well good, because you would've had to fight me for the pink one," she said with a wink and flipped the green one to Maya who caught it with a grin.

"Thanks for coming," she said.

I looked between them, startled. "You invited her?" I asked Maya, confused.

Lexi arched an eyebrow at me, "Do I need an invitation?"

"Of course not!" I rushed out, but stopped when I saw the laughter in her eyes. She was like a sister to me and knew she was always welcome.

I rolled my eyes at her, she grinned before turning back to Maya, her face growing more serious when she met Maya's eyes. "Anything for Savannah. Speaking of which," she said, eyes rounding back on me, "when exactly were you going to tell me how bad things had gotten over at Hedge Fund?"

I paled. It wasn't that I was hiding it from her per se, but there was nothing she could do about it. "I didn't want you to feel useless."

She pursed her lips and leveled a stare at me that made me swallow the rest of my words.

"The only way I can be useless is if you don't use me." Her voice softened as she said, "Sav, you know I love you and would do anything for you." I nodded. "So not only are you not signing that new contract, but we're going to figure out how to break the current one."

"But... I can't," I protested, not daring to let myself hope. "I'm not sure what Maya told you, but they threatened to go public about me and Maya if I don't sign."

She grinned, "Let them. Once you go public with the recording Maya told me you have, your fans won't believe a word they say and will be boycotting the label for bi-erasure."

"Unless you don't think we can be convincing?" Maya said with a mischievous grin. "I think you're quite convincing about being attracted to me."

I laughed at that as she said, "I know I make it easy," and she winked at me.

Lexi looked back and forth between us before quirking an eyebrow at me, but said nothing.

"If that's your only objection, then we should get to work," Maya nodded at Lexi, "we have loopholes to find."

I moved to the table and saw we were looking at copies of my current contract. "I don't get it. Even if I'm not signing a new contract with them, that won't get me out of my old one."

"That's why we're looking for loopholes," Lexi said easily.

"But why? They already have my newest album, once it releases, I'll be done with them." I almost couldn't believe it after yesterday, but they were right. Of course they were, my freedom was worth fighting for and I had loyal fans who would stand by my side. If I hadn't known that before, the showing to my Pride performance had solidified that.

"Well, I want to make sure there's nothing in here that lets them pull you back in," Lexi explained and I paled at the thought. There couldn't be, was there? The more I considered it, the more likely it seemed, but Lexi had read it before, if there were something in there, she would have caught it. "I know," she said, answering my look, "I'm almost positive there's nothing hidden in here we haven't seen before, but before we make our move, I want to be positive. Besides, I'm hoping there's a way to get you your latest album back."

I teared up looking between the two of them, daring to let myself hope. "Is that actually possible?" All of my work was important to me, but this album was especially important. My entire heart and soul were bared in it. It was a funeral for my marriage and a celebration of my freedom, of my divorce aptly named Rising From the Ashes. In truth, I hated the idea of Hedge Fund Records owning any part of it.

"I'm not sure," Lexi said.

"But if there is, we'll find it," Maya finished, pulling out a chair for me. I quickly sat with a smile that I hoped conveyed my gratitude to them both and pulled a contract copy to me. They did the same as we settled in for a long day.

A couple of hours later, Maya broke the silence, "I think I have an idea."

"You do?" I asked quickly as Lexi said, "well what is it?"

"She has to deliver a last album to them, and you have already, right?"

I nodded. The album had been finished and turned in to them weeks ago. It came out in 3 short weeks, even if I wanted to there was no way to take it back now.

"So that part is done, they'll have their album, but nowhere in there does it say how long you have to wait before putting out a new album after that." She grinned triumphantly. "They probably imagined you would either be signed back on with them or that you wouldn't be important enough for them to care anymore, but fortunately for us, neither of those is true. Their bad planning is our gain."

I was starting to see where she was going with that, "So you think I should start working on my next album?"

She nodded, "I do. I think you need an album of your own to compete with theirs."

"It'll take a while to have something like that produced and ready to go," Lexi said what I was thinking. I had been working on some new songs but only a couple were ready to go. There was no way I could have something ready in three weeks.

"I can't work that fast. I can't write all new songs that quickly, and do you really think competing with my other album is the way to go?"

"What if you didn't have to write all new songs? What if you had help? Besides, nowhere in the contract does it say you have to promote their album or that it has to do well."

I frowned at that, "You don't want it to do well? I know Hedge Fund is awful, but I put my heart into that album. I know my fans are going to love it and I want it to do well."

"Actually," she said with a gleam in her eye, "you put your heart and soul into those songs."

"Same thing," I said, confused.

"Not at all, an album is its songs, but songs are not an album."

"What?" I asked, not even pretending to follow her logic. I looked over at Lexi to see a slow smile spread across her face.

"They own the album," she said slowly, "not the songs."

I wrinkled my brow, "Aren't those the same thing?"

Lexi was still looking at Maya, "you're right. You're a damn genius, that would work."

"What would work?" I asked, frustration waring with confusion in my tone.

"You don't have to write all new songs," Maya said her grin wide as she explained, "you can rerecord the songs you wrote for the album."

"Then there would be two albums?" I asked, still not understanding. "Why would that help?"

"If you give your fans an alternative and a reason not to support your old label, they'll buy your version," Lexi said considering. "Those bastards at Hegde Fund are going to out you and Maya's fake relationship anyway, you have no reason not to tell your fans they're bigots who want to force you back in the closet and back to an unhappy, faithless marriage."

"You really think they would believe me? That they would support me?"

"They love you, not your record label." Lexi said nodding.

"Besides," Maya said, "the millisecond the queer community hears about how you're being treated, they'll boycott the label and rush out in droves to buy your version. Especially because we're going to make it gay as fuck."

I laughed at that, "What do you mean?"

She considered a moment, "Rainbow albums obviously."

I laughed, "of course," like that was the most natural thing in the world, but as she said it, I could picture it. A rainbow phoenix rising from the ashes in printed in the middle and the albums and vinyl themselves would be rainbow colored instead of silver. I loved it already.

"And queer features of course. Do you think Miss Lucy has a singing voice?"

I shrugged, "I have no idea."

She considered, "Well if she doesn't, she'll still shine in a music video."

I laughed at that.

"So, you want me to rerecord a gayer version of Rising from the Ashes in three weeks?"

She nodded, "Not only that, but I want you to reach out to all your queer industry friends to see who can squeeze a feature into their schedule."

"It's such short notice though," I said. I hating imposing on others and this was a big ask.

Lexi laughed at that and Maya said, "anyone who wouldn't drop their schedule to feature on your album is insane in my book."

"Anyone?" I asked, an idea forming.

"Anyone." She agreed with conviction.

"So, am I picking your feature or do you want to?"

The stunned look on her face, slowly replaced by wonder had me grinning, "You want me?"

"You said I could pick anyone, and you're my first pick."

Her smile widened, "Are you sure?" she asked softly.

"Very sure, you're my first round draft pick and you're not getting out of this."

"I wouldn't dream of it," she said lacing her fingers through mine, "now pull up the track list and we'll get to planning."

"Elle Emerson would probably do it." I startled at Lexi's voice. I had managed to forget she was here and I blushed when I saw her look pointedly at my hand intertwined with Maya's, but again she didn't say anything. The look she shot me told me I would be answering to her later for it though. Mercifully though, she just looked back down at her phone and proceeded to name other contacts we could try while Maya pulled hers out and started a list.

After a couple more hours we had secured 6 queer artists to feature on my 13 songs. They would only have to be minisculely reworked to fit in the feature and I was grateful we weren't making much more work. Especially since I had decided to add the three new songs I had written. They were much gayer than my previous works and would fit the new album perfectly. It was going to be hard work, but the vision for Rising from the Ashes: the Rainbow Version was already forming in my mind and I couldn't wait to see it come to fruition. I had no idea how I was going to finish the rerecords in time for vinyl and albums to be printed, but Lexi told me to leave that to her. There was nothing she couldn't do and I didn't envy whoever she was going to contact to help her make it happen.

The next few weeks was going to be crazy between Elite's plans for us and the rerecords and I hoped we would have enough time for everything. I thought maybe I could get Clarice to go easy on us if she saw how well we were working together. It was no small miracle in and of itself for me and Maya to be working so well together, and I wouldn't have believed it myself a few short weeks ago, but I was incredibly grateful to the hell that I had gone through for bringing her back into my life. I hadn't expected to ever have her back, and I wouldn't have dreamed how our relationship would have evolved and gotten physical, but I was grateful for whatever it was we were doing. I didn't really know how she felt or what it was I was feeling, but I was happy for the time I had with her.

I felt happier, lighter with her around. If I was the phoenix rising from the ashes, she was the sun that warmed my flight and I basked in her rays.

Chapter 30

Savannah

After explaining the situation to Clarice and a quick conference call into Elite with me, Lexi, Maya and Clarice all sitting around my table, they agreed to flexibility and letting us take this week mostly off to record, provided we were seen with at least two of my guest features out in public that week.

It was an easy compromise and we all quickly agreed. Most of the featured artists were friends of mine anyway and the idea of getting to spend more time with them made me happy.

It turned out the band had a lot more questions than Elite did. When I called a team facetime, they were all so upset that I was letting the company treat me like that. I almost turned my camera off so they wouldn't see my tears, but didn't. I didn't hide from them. Connor and Stevie were family. Nikki was newer and we were still getting to know each other, but Stevie loved her and that was good enough for me. None of them gave me a hard time about the increased work we were going to have to do. They were all down to eat, sleep and breath Rising From the Ashes: the Rainbow Version for the next week. I was incredibly grateful for them all and made sure they knew I couldn't have done this with anyone else.

HOLLYWOOD'S GIRLS NIGHT OUT

Iconic, or should we say bi-conic pop legend Savannah Hollywood has been spotted out on the town with her girlfriend Maya Ryder. They were so wrapped up in each other they barely noticed the cameras. We have exclusive never before seen photos, and look at how in love they look. Maya looks at Savannah like she's the goddess she is. What surprises us is how Savannah looks at her like she's the moon and the stars. We pulled some old pictures of her and Darren Dawson and can't find a single one of her looking at him like that for the entire 8 years they were together.

We don't know about you all, but we're happy to see her so happy. It's interesting that Darren hasn't been seen out and about lately. People are saying he's busy filming his new movie, but we wonder if he's been hiding his face on purpose. If we were him, we would be sorely regretting what's sure to be the biggest fumble in all of history. He was married to Savannah freaking Hollywood and he let her get away. If we were him, we wouldn't be showing our faces out on the town either.

Speaking of being out on the town, Savannah and Maya were spotted getting buddy buddy with some other famous faces you'll recognize. Click on the link to find out who and see the photos.

Chapter 31

Savannah

I hadn't seen much of Maya for the week. I was holed up with my band in my basement studio recording and rerecording the songs, so Clarice let her go visit her grandma in the mornings as long as she was back here by the afternoon.

It was weird not spending every minute with her like I was used to, but even weirder that this new pattern seemed to better mimic what our lives would be like if this were real. She would be leaving to go to work and we would spend the evenings and nights together. Her brief absences were making it even clearer to me that I wanted her around for real and I hadn't the faintest clue if she felt the same or what to do about it. Luckily, I had four more weeks with her to figure things out. I could only hope things got easier or at the very least that I figured out what I was feeling and what to do about it.

CHAPTER 32

MAYA

My grandma hadn't forgotten Savannah from back in the day and had so many questions for me. I tried to tell her it wasn't a big deal, but she didn't let that slide.

"Not a big deal? My granddaughter is dating-"

"We're not really dating," I quickly interrupted, "It's just a publicity stunt." Saying it felt sour on my tongue, but it was the truth. Sure, things had changed between us, and whatever it was we were doing meant more to me than I had imagined it would, but we weren't actually together.

She gave me a dubious look before continuing, "Okay, my granddaughter is *fake dating*" she emphasized fake dating with air quotes that had me rolling my eyes, "her old best friend who happens to be one of the most famous women in the world, and you're telling me it's not a big deal?"

"Cynthia from the bridge club called to ask me about it and Nancy on the corner stopped by with a magazine asking if it was you. The neighborhood and the senior center and even my book club ladies have been talking non-stop about my famous gay grand-daughter." She grinned at that, "That'll show Evelyn.

Always bragging about her grandson who's a doctor. Well, I have a famous granddaughter. Take that."

I burst out laughing at that. "Gram, it's not really a big deal."

"Sweetheart, everyone is talking about you! And besides, it's Sav and nothing between you and her will ever not be a big deal."

"What do you mean?" I asked.

She shrugged, "I thought it was obvious how you felt about each other. I had never seen you so hurt or betrayed then you were when things ended badly with her. I tried and tried to get you to talk to her, but you wouldn't listen. You needed to heal and work through your pain, and I understand that, but" she cupped my face in her hands and said softly, "but my darling girl, look at how happy you are now."

I was struggling to process what she was saying. "We were just friends back then."

Her eyes were shining when she looked at me, "Oh sweetie, whatever you need to tell yourself."

I thought back for a moment to how things were with her. We were incredibly close back then, sure, but there weren't any feelings, were there? Sure, I spent more time with her than I did with anyone else in my life and I loved her fiercely, but as a best friend. We had come out to each other, but she never had any interest in me and I wasn't interested in her more than anyone else with. Anyone with a pulse knew how gorgeous Sav was, there was no denying it, but I respected her and our friendship too much to have had actual feelings.

Now, looking back though, it was easy to see how quickly I would have blurred those lines if she had wanted to.

"I'm just happy to have her back in my life," I said finally.

"And I'm happy for you too, sweetie. Will I get to see her sometime soon?"

"Hopefully, she's super busy though so I don't know when," but I knew Sav would try to make time. She loved my Gram almost as much as I did.

"Who's coming over?" I heard my sister's loud voice call from behind us and then heard a screech. I turned around just in time to catch my little niece Kat as she flew at me yelling "Auntie! Auntie Maya!"

I got down on my knees to give her a giant hug. When she pulled away, she was grinning wide and turned around, "Mama! Mama! Auntie Maya's here!"

Leslie grinned at her little girl, "Yes she is," she waved to me and I beamed at her. I had missed them both so much. It had only been a few weeks but I missed them both fiercely.

"Why don't you show Auntie Maya what you made for her?"

She patted down her pockets and looked alarmed when she came up empty, she looked back to her mom with worry in her eyes that quickly faded into excitement when she saw the folded up piece of paper my sister was holding. She ran and grabbed it and quickly brought it over to me.

I opened it and saw two brightly colored stick figures, one with parrot like purple hair and I chuckled, "Kitty Kat, is that me?" I asked pointed at the purple one.

She nodded watching me solemnly, waiting.

"I love it! You're such a good artist!"

She grinned and before I could ask, she pointed at the other figure, "and that's Auntie Savannah!"

"Auntie Savannah?" I sputtered out, glaring at my sister over Kat's head.

Leslie looked guilty but not remorseful and just shrugged.

Kat didn't catch our exchange and said, "She's super super pretty! And Mama says she's super smart and talented. When I grow up I wanna be just like her!"

That put the smile back on my face. There were definitely worse people for her to look up to.

"And I love her songs. She has such a pretty voice!"

At this I turned another accusing look to Leslie who again shrugged. "She's all over the radio."

I felt a pang of betrayal roll over me at the admission that she had been listening to Sav's music, especially since she didn't know the details of our reconciliation, but I tried to remind myself that Sav had been her friend too. She had been a second sister to Leslie and Leslie had been loyal to me back then, but I knew it had hurt her too. I really hoped I could get Sav out here to visit soon. I was positive she missed Leslie and Gram as much as they had missed her. She had been a permanent fixture around here for a long time.

Gram took Kat's hand and said, "Why don't you come help Grammy in the kitchen, Kitty Kat?"

"But I wanna hang out with Auntie Maya," she complained. It saddened me and warmed my heart at the same time.

"I'll be here for a while, kiddo," I assured her.

She looked at me seriously and asked, "Pinky promise?"

I made a show of considering before nodding solemnly and giving her my pinky.

She shook it with a nod and turned back to Gram, "Okay, I'll come."

Gram leaned down and stage whispered, "Perfect, because my chocolate chip cookies aren't going to eat themselves."

Kat squealed and raced out of the living room with Gram trailing behind her.

Leslie looked at me and said, "sooo, you're dating Savannah freaking Hollywood," she says with a low whistle.

I roll my eyes, "We're not actually dating." I said for the second time that day, not feeling like I was any more convincing this time.

Leslie quirked an eyebrow at me, "I've seen the pictures. Neither of you are that good of actresses."

"Hey!"

She held her hands up in mock defeat laughing, "Okay, okay. That's not what I meant. You're a phenomenal actress, but that wasn't acting and you know it. Besides this is Sav we're talking about."

I sighed, "Yeah, it's Sav."

"How is she anyway? I heard about the divorce and her latest single was a dozy. Kat won't listen to it. She says she doesn't like anything that makes me cry."

I winced at that, but Leslie just waved a hand at me, "I'm okay, please don't worry. Just hit home a little harder than I expected with the divorce, that's all."

I nodded, understanding what she meant. I hadn't been through anything like that, and even I could admit the song was heartbreaking. "She's doing okay. She'll be better once the asshat is officially out of her life, but she's dealing."

"I'm glad she has you."

I shrugged at that, "she has a lot of people."

Leslie shook her head, "maybe she does. I don't know Sav anymore, but I did know our Sav and I know how much you meant to each other. It wouldn't matter if she was surrounded by loving, supportive people, which I hope she is but with how much her family sucked, I'm skeptical. But yeah, it wouldn't matter how many people were there for her, she would still want you there."

"There's nothing special about me," I said, but her words both broke and touched my heart. I was glad to be back in Sav's life, but it was killing me that I had spent so much time punishing her and myself for the past. That I had been selfish enough to keep her from Gram and Leslie too, from the only family she had. I didn't know how she wanted me, but I was sure I didn't deserve her.

Leslie leveled a look at me that had me feeling like I was in trouble and said, "Maya Jane Ryder, I won't hear you say anything mean about my favorite sister."

It was an old inside joke of ours that we only pulled out occasionally as it was guaranteed to make the other one smile. I was her only sister.

"And your least favorite," I answered smiling.

"Always," she said smiling too. Until her face grew serious and she said, "But seriously, you were a life-saver to me and Kat. You got me through the divorce emotionally and financially. I have no idea where Kat and I would have been then or now without your help. Gram too, you're always here for her. You're an angel with spiky purple hair and a leather jacket." I chuckled at that but she wasn't done. "I'm so lucky to have you as my sister. I love you and our little family so much. Sav's lucky to have you in her life. You might not see how much you help the people around you but I do and she's damn lucky. I would say I hope she knows it, but it's Sav so I know she does."

I smiled at that, "She's good to me too. Plus," I added thoughtfully, "with this job, if we're careful with the money, none of us would have to work again."

Her eyes widened, "you can't be serious? You're getting that much?"

I considered a moment and amended, "Well, Kat would have to work someday, but her college is paid for or if she doesn't want to go to school, she'll have a nice little nest egg to get her started. I already set up a trust fund for her. It can't be touched until after she graduates high school, but it's hers."

Leslie's eyes were wide as saucers, "You can't be serious."

I nodded, "Of course I am. I don't have all the money yet, but it'll be enough to take care of anything and everything Gram could ever want or need. Enough to support me through jobs, because I'm gonna get a kick ass acting job after this, and enough to support you and Kat for as long as you want. If you didn't want to work, you wouldn't have to."

I looked up and saw tears streaming down her face, "Maya," she said through what had now turned to gasping sobs, "you don't have to do that."

I pulled her tight into me cradling her head into my shoulder and said, "I know I don't have to, but I want to. I got ridiculously lucky with this job, like won the Hollywood lottery lucky, and I want to share the wealth. Besides when I get rich and famous from my next acting gig, I'll have way more money than I know what to do with."

She was still crying but I felt her smile against my shoulder.

Kat barreled back into the room followed closely by Gram, "Mama, are you okay?" Kat asked in a small concerned voice.

I let go of Leslie and she smiled broadly at Kat while wiping away some of her tears, "I'm okay sweetie, come here," she held out her arms for Kat who flew into her hug.

"Auntie Maya just gave Mama some really really good news. These are happy tears."

Kat pulled back, inspecting Leslie's face before nodding. "That's good! Dance party time?"

Leslie looked sheepishly at me before pulling out her phone and queuing up a song. She nodded to Kat "Definitely dance party time."

I didn't recognize the song itself but the singer was unmistakably Sav. It was a fast paced pop song of hers I hadn't heard in a long time. It used to be on the radio constantly. I used to have to go out of my way to avoid it, it had been everywhere. Now, dancing around the living room with my sister, little niece, and Gram, I couldn't help loving the song.

On the way home, I cued up some of her old songs that I never let myself listen to. I drove to the soundtrack of Sav singing her heart out about love and loss, happiness and tragedy. I found myself liking the happy songs and love songs the best. I especially loved the hearing her sharp little inhales before a challenging note or line. They gave me very vivid memories of what she sounded like below me.

The thoughts made the drive go by torturously slowly, but I was grateful Sav was winding down on the re-recording project so we would have a night off. Tomorrow we were back to work, starting rehearsals for her album release concert, but tonight it would be just me and her and I intended to make her make more of her sharp little inhales.

Chapter 33

Savannah

Nervous didn't begin to cover how I was feeling about Maya spending time with the band, about singing one of my new songs with her. I thought I was too seasoned to get nervous about performances like this, but apparently, I was wrong. My nerves were through the roof and we hadn't even started practicing yet.

It made sense with how monumental the stakes were. I was openly bisexual, performing with my girlfriend and announcing my newest album all as a giant "Fuck you" to Hedge Fund Records. It needed to be perfect. I needed to be perfect. Besides that, there was the added complication of Maya.

It wasn't just the performance itself that was stressing me out, it was the *performance*. Having to show just the right amount of feelings for Maya, just enough chemistry and feeling that it was believable, but not too much. Just enough so that when Maya went through with our contractually obligated break up in a few weeks, my fans would be disappointed but not devastated. I was another story altogether. Just thinking about our relationship being on a deadline had my stomach in knots, so I was trying not to think about it. Instead, I was pouring myself into my work and I definitely wasn't thinking about Maya's hands on me. I wasn't thinking about her smile and how safe I felt with her. And I definitely wasn't thinking about how my house had never felt like a home until she moved in.

I was in the danger zone and needed to proceed with caution; I knew that, but it was so hard to be cautious with her. She was fire, and I knew how this would end, but I would follow her to hell. She was worth burning for.

I hadn't felt this much passion in a long time, if ever. She brought out a side of me I couldn't help but love. Maybe it was her, or maybe it was the divorce, but I hadn't felt this much like myself in a long time. I felt like I was rediscovering myself when I didn't even know I had lost her.

I had been with Darren so long that it was hard to see things objectively, but I had been anxious for a long time, holding my breath, worried I would say the wrong thing or that something would set him off. He would never tell me what upset him, would never talk to me about things before blowing up.

Clearly, things were different with Maya. She didn't pull any punches. She was the first to tell me exactly what she was thinking; she was nothing if not direct. I admired that about her. I was always changing how I acted and what I said to cater to the people around me. Maybe that came from being famous or maybe it was me, but there was no doubt that I cared a little too much about what other people thought of me. It was refreshing to be around someone like Maya who clearly couldn't care less what people thought about her. I had always loved that about her.

I glanced at the clock and, with a sense of dread, saw that it was time to head over to our first rehearsal. There was a reason I had been keeping Maya away from the rest of the crew. Originally, I was worried they would see right through me, especially Connor. I didn't think there was any way I could convince him that I even liked Maya never mind that I was actually dating her. I wanted to tell him the truth, but Lexi was right when she said the fewer people that knew, the better. Originally, I was worried he would know I hated her, but now things were more complicated. My feelings were messy. Now I didn't know what he'd see, but I was sure it would be too much.

CHAPTER 34

MAYA

I was surprised at how easy it still was to sing with her. Our voices harmonized together just right. I shouldn't have been surprised. After all, that wasn't the only way we fit well together.

Yes, it was a bad idea. I knew she would drop me again the second I became an inconvenience, but damn if I wasn't willing to enjoy her until then. I wanted her, in more ways than one, but I would take her however she would have me. The way her drummer, Connor, was smirking at me, I wondered if there was any truth to the rumors about her and him, if he knew her the way I did. The thought wasn't one I liked.

I thought we would be there for maybe an hour, but apparently Hollywood ran a tighter ship than I thought. If it had just been me she critiqued, I might have taken it personally, but she had notes for everyone.

After her telling Connor his tempo was off for the fifth time, I leaned over and whispered to her bassist, "Is she always like this?"

The bassist, Stevie, brushed her blue bangs away from her face and grinned. "No, she's normally worse."

I had to laugh. I swallowed most of the chuckle, but Hollywood heard me. She glared at me, which made me laugh harder. Stevie started laughing, too.

Hollywood rolled her eyes and huffed at me. "What's so funny?"

I raised an eyebrow at her. "You."

Stevie laughed harder at that. I could see Nikki behind the keyboard trying not to laugh. Hollywood glared at me a moment, but the way her nose scrunched up when she was angry was too adorable for me to take her seriously.

Connor sucked in a breath and said, "Careful there, Maya, your girl isn't known to take jokes well before performances."

"Just before performances?" Stevie added through her laughter.

"Hey! Come on you guys, you're supposed to be my friends."

"And as your friends, we need you to know if we didn't love you as much as we do, there is no way in hell we could work with you."

"Come on, guys, I'm not that bad," she said, hitting them with a look that dared him to disagree.

No one did, but after a moment, she threw her hands up in the air and moved across the room, turning her back to us. There was something about the movement that told me she wasn't messing around. This, whatever it was, was serious.

I was across the room at her side before I noticed I had moved, and then blinked and noticed Connor had moved, too. I looked at him, surprised for a moment, before taking a step back. Of course he was here. He'd been through a lot with her and he'd been there for her. I didn't know why I thought for a moment that she needed me.

He looked at me, confused, and mirrored my step back, gesturing to me to go to her. I shook my head and nodded at him. It was his place, not mine. Even if I knew what to say or how to comfort her or even what was wrong, I knew she would choose Connor over me. She was closer with him and would want his comfort over mine. What I wanted didn't matter right now, just that Sav was okay, so I stayed put.

While we were silently arguing about who should go to her, she stood there with her head in her hands. "I just want everything to be perfect," she said softly.

The defeat in her voice almost made me sink to my knees. Hollywood was worried about being perfect? Of course the performance was going to be perfect. Part of the reason she drove me so crazy was that every damn thing the woman did was perfect.

"Of course it will be," I said.

Stevie sauntered up and elbowed Connor, saying, "I don't know if there's any amount of practice that could fix your tempo problems."

"Hey! There's nothing wrong with my tempo," he said, shouldering her back, but Stevie stepped out of his way, moving toward Hollywood so quickly he almost toppled over.

Stevie crossed to Hollywood's side and put her hands on her, gently turning her around. She held out her arms for a hug, but to everyone's surprise, Hollywood moved past Stevie and Connor and launched herself into my arms. I barely had time to catch my balance and keep us from toppling over, but somehow, I managed.

She felt smaller in my arms than usual, and I hated the way she was shaking.

"It'll be amazing. You have nothing to worry about," I told her, holding her tight. I couldn't imagine how much pressure she was under right now with the crap with Hedge Fund Records, her divorce, and now her newest album. It was a lot for one person to handle, but if anyone could handle it, it was her. I held her tightly, surprised but happy to have her in my arms.

I wasn't sure what surprised me more, that she sought me out for comfort or how happy Connor and Stevie looked at seeing her wrapped in my arms. Nikki gave me a little thumbs up from behind her keyboard. Connor came over and clapped me on the back, putting his arms around the both of us.

A moment later, Stevie skipped over, saying, "Hey you can't leave me out," and squeezed herself into what was now an unasked for group hug. "Get over here, sweetheart," she called out and Nikki scooted out from behind her keys and hugged Stevie from behind, joining us.

Hollywood nuzzled her head onto my shoulder, and I met Connor's eye over her head. He looked at her and smiled at me, squeezing us tighter, and my heart soared. I had been telling myself their opinions didn't matter, but having the approval of the people I knew she considered her family made me happy in a way I wasn't ready to begin to examine, because the second I thought about it, I was having to chase away the creeping guilt about lying to them, about this being fake.

Or at least, it *was* fake. I wasn't sure what it was anymore. Was it still fake or was I lying to myself? There was real potential for one of us to really get hurt, and I was starting to get worried because I knew just how badly walking away from Savannah had hurt the first time and knew it would be exponentially worse this time.

Hollywood High's It Couple Gets Hot and Heavy

Savannah Hollywood was spotted cozying up with none other than Maya Ryder. For those of you that don't remember, Savannah and Maya played on screen rivals in Savannah's hit show, Hollywood High. The show was a home run until Hollywood outgrew it. She moved on from acting and made her big break in the music scene, moving her and Maya from on-screen rivals to real life rivals.

They took the world by storm earlier this week, revealing that not only have they set aside their differences and buried the hatchet, but now they're dating.

It's no secret that Maya identifies as a lesbian, but Savannah Hollywood coming out as bisexual was a shock to the world, and it seems like the girls are far from done shocking us.

From roller-skating in the park, to candlelight dinners on the town, to getting down and dirty on the beach, these girls have not been messing around, or rather they've been messing around with each other and seem to be going full throttle into their relationship.

From their amount of public outings, it seems Savannah isn't shying away from making a statement.

Savannah isn't letting anything get in her way of being happy, least of all her husband and the not yet signed divorce papers.

Sources say that Savannah has tried to get his signature on a separation agreement numerous times but that he keeps insisting on higher alimony. Sources also say she has been trying to serve him with divorce papers and a court date, but hasn't been able to pin him down. This reporter can't help but wonder whose shoulder he might be crying on and what a girl would have to do to be so lucky.

Chapter 35

Savannah

The week passed in a whirlwind of rehearsals and staged public dates. I was exhausted and relieved when Clarice and Elite threw us a bone, letting me and Maya go back to Rizzo's to the same private table we had a few short weeks ago. It was supposed to be a relaxing dinner, but the entire ride there I was wound up thinking about the last time we had been there and how much had changed. This time, when we got home from the date, I would be taking her to bed instead of going to bed frustrated.

I was thinking about what the night back home would bring us and couldn't keep the flush from my face. Walking to our table, I felt Maya's eyes on me and knew from her smirk that she was thinking the same. I couldn't stop thinking about her touch and how well she knew my body. It didn't help that now that we were back at Rizzo's, I couldn't help thinking about how hot our dinner was here the last time. We had both gotten carried away, but it was so easy to get lost in her, in the taste of her tongue. In the feel of her lips against mine.

When we were seated and Antonio shut the door, I felt her eyes jump to mine, and then felt them trail down my body. My tongue darted nervously across my lips and her eyes flew back up to watch. I could feel my heart quicken when I saw her eyes darken with need. It was exhilarating knowing I wasn't the only one who couldn't think straight.

I felt my body flush and let myself take in the black number she was wearing. Her leather corset top hugged her curves in a way that was hard to tear your eyes from. Under the table, I knew she was wearing a long black skirt with a slit on the right side that had captured my attention most of the night.

I looked at her with a feeling of anticipation, wondering if this was going to be anything like last time. I tried to convince myself I didn't want it to be like last time, but I wasn't a good enough liar, not even to myself.

Antonio came back in and asked what we would be having this evening. I went to answer and had to suck in a gasp when I felt a hand on my thigh. *Fuck*. I tried to concentrate, but her thumb started stroking circles on my thigh and I was struggling to breathe.

Her hand started making its way further north, and I had never been more thankful to have a usual order. With Antonio's watchful eyes on me, all I had to ground out was, "The usual."

I stifled a gasp as best I could when I felt her hand slip under my dress.

I hoped it would escape Antonio's notice, but I should have known better. He was observant. He cocked his head to the side, watching me with concern. "Are you okay, Miss Hollywood?" he asked.

I bit my lip and nodded. He scrutinized me another moment. I held my breath as she stroked my inner thigh, not daring to breathe. Not trusting what noises might come out of my mouth.

It wasn't until I heard her breathy chuckle that I realized I had moved my thighs further apart, instinctually giving her more access. I was thankful the tablecloth covered her hand, but if she kept it up much longer, I was done for. From the smirk on her face, she knew just what she was doing to me.

She ordered without batting an eye. If I wasn't currently on the receiving end of her touch, I wouldn't have the slightest clue she was at all distracted.

As she neared my panties, I prayed to the universe that Antonio would leave. There was no way in hell I could keep my composure if she kept going. Would she keep going? It wouldn't be the first time, but we were in public. She wouldn't really do that in public, would she? Would I let her? I wasn't sure about anything, but my skin was on fire and I was aching for her touch.

By the grace of the universe, when Maya pushed my panties to the side and ran her finger down my slit, he turned on his heel and left. A small mercy since not a moment after the door closed behind him, she plunged a finger inside of me, and I let out a breathy moan.

Her eyes widened for a moment before a grin settled on her face. "Damn, if I knew how wet you were for me, I would've done something about it sooner."

I felt fireworks go off when she simultaneously slid a second finger in me and stroked my clit with her thumb. I bit my lip to keep the moan from escaping and failed.

"Better keep quiet. Wouldn't want anyone to think you might be enjoying yourself."

I blushed deeper and felt her start to withdraw. She let out a throaty laugh when I ground against her, not wanting the pleasure to stop.

She smirked at me. "My little exhibitionist."

She was right. I should care that we were out in public, in my favorite restaurant, and that Antonio could come back at any time. I shouldn't be enjoying this, never mind encouraging it, but I couldn't bring myself to stop grinding against her, couldn't bring myself to want her to stop.

I should be terrified of being found out, terrified of someone hearing and guessing what was going on between me and my very public girlfriend, but I wasn't. The adrenaline coursing through my system at the thought of being caught made it that much hotter.

Not that I would admit that to her even if I could make my mouth form a response, but with her fingers working inside of me, my thoughts were barely coherent. I let out another low moan and watched her eyes dance over me.

"How about we see how loud you can really get?" she said before slipping her fingers out of me.

I whimpered, instantly feeling the loss of her, feeling empty without her inside of me. I pouted at her for half a moment before she stunned me into silence by ducking under the table.

"What are you doing?" I whispered. and a moment later, gasped when I felt her push my thighs further apart.

"What the hell are you doing?" I asked quickly, fighting to keep control of myself. She couldn't be doing what I thought she was going to. We were in a god damn restaurant, a private room, but still.

There was little room for doubt when I felt her pull my panties down my legs.

I heard her chuckle. "Leopard print? Really?"

With her fingers trailing along my inner thighs, it took me longer than it should have to understand her meaning.

I blushed. "They're cute. Besides, I didn't think it would matter. I didn't think you'd be looking."

It was a lie and we both knew it. I knew she'd see them, I just didn't think it would be until after the restaurant.

I gasped, feeling her tongue run the length of my lips before circling my clit, and then pulling back.

"If I knew you'd react like this, I would have done this ages ago," she breathed out.

I could feel the warmth of her breath, how close she was to where I so desperately wanted her. It took all my restraint to not reach down and lace my fingers through her hair. I wanted this, badly, but we were in a restaurant, for fuck's sake. We were celebrities in a god damn restaurant and we couldn't be doing this, at least not here.

"I want this, god, do I want this-" I started.

"Don't bring god into this. I want to hear my name on your lips."

With that, she pushed her tongue past my folds and the feel of her inside me made me struggle not to cry out. A few moments later, I cried out when she inserted a finger in me and licked her way back up to my clit. When she sucked on it, I couldn't stop myself from moaning her name.

She pulled back, and I whimpered. The tablecloth fully covered her, but I could hear her smirk when she said, "Good girl". She stuck a second finger into me and I groaned, grinding against her. I moved one of my hands to her head, needing her tongue on me, but she pulled away again.

"Baby, we're doing this my way or not at all. Either sit or your hands or make them useful and play with your tits for me."

I didn't have to be told twice. I moved my hands up to my breasts and started to squeeze them. When

I brushed over my nipples, I shivered, feeling how hard they were. My backless dress didn't leave room for a bra, so it was just the thin fabric between my hands and my nipples. The way the fabric was rubbing against them made me grind against Maya's tongue and fingers even harder.

I felt her pull away again and almost reached for her, but stopped myself just in time, remembering her rule. Maybe she wasn't serious, but this felt too damned good to test that.

"I think the waiter's coming back. Better hurry up and finish there, Sav."

Fuck. The restaurant; we were in a god damn restaurant and Antonio was coming back.

How I had managed to forget that was beyond me, but with her tongue and fingers on me, I barely remembered my own name.

She started tonguing my clit again, alternating between flicking it and suckling on it. With two of her fingers moving inside of me, I was on the edge and she knew it. She was moving her fingers infuriatingly slowly and, to make matters worse, pulled away every time I tried to grind against her. I was helplessly riding the ebb and flow of pleasure she was dealing out. I didn't know what she was waiting for, but I was desperate for release, desperate for her to give it to me.

I moaned loudly when she sped up her rhythm. I was so close, so close I just barely heard the door open.

I tried to close my thighs, but she held them apart, continuing her assault.

I nudged her with my foot, but she didn't stop.

I fought to hold in a moan at my building pleasure while Antonio looked at Maya's empty place.

He set her plate down infuriately slow; I bit my tongue, trying to keep from crying out. I could taste blood in my mouth, but even that didn't halt the climax I could feel building.

When he turned to me and quirked an eyebrow, I couldn't decide if it was because I was doing a terrible job of hiding things or because he was wondering where Maya had gone. I prayed it was the latter and forced out, "Bathroom," as nonchalantly as I could.

He seemed skeptical, but thankfully just nodded and placed my plate in front of me.

He turned to leave, but a gasp slipped from my lips as she increased her assault. I was going to kill her if I didn't die from embarrassment and pleasure first.

He turned around, and I managed to push out, "Thank you."

He looked at me a moment longer before pushing open the door and shutting it behind him. Not a moment too soon since her gently brushing her teeth over my clit sent me careening over the edge. In desperation, I bit down on my hand, trying to keep the cries from coming out.

She kept moving her fingers inside me, making me ride out my climax, but thankfully she slowed as the waves of pleasure raced through me. Only stopping when I finally breathed out, "Fuck, Maya."

I flipped the table skirt up to get a look at her, but she had already moved back and emerged on her side of the table.

"Dinner smells delicious," she looked at me with a glint in her eye and slowly raised her fingers to her lips, saying, "but you're much sweeter," before sucking on each of her fingers slowly, savoring the taste of me.

"I've always been a dessert first kind of girl," she said, and made a show of considering before adding, "and after."

When she winked, I felt my body heat up again, and my face flushed. As we ate our dinner, I couldn't help thinking about everything I wanted to do to her and have her do to me the second I got her home.

HOLLYWOOD'S OLD FLAME MEETS HER NEW BEAU

Savannah Hollywood and Maya Ryder were spotted getting cozy at Rizzo's yet again. While it's not surprising Savannah loves to frequent the place, her audacity in bringing her new beau around her old flame was nothing short of shocking.

Not only did she parade Maya in front of the waiter she used to date, but sources say the poor man had to wait on them all night. Savannah isn't known for being cruel, but we can't help but wonder if there's something to the things her soon-to-be ex-husband Darren Dawson has been saying about her, but only time will tell.

HOLLYWOOD'S CHART TOPPING ALBUM IS SET TO MAKE HEADLINES

Savannah Hollywood's latest album releases tomorrow. There has been so much speculation about just what Savannah and her team have planned for the launch, but we finally know the where. She's taking over the Hollywood Bowl and playing her latest album for everyone lucky enough to have scored tickets.

The tickets were gone within seconds, an unheard-of feat for an unprecedented event. Only Savannah Hollywood would throw a full impromptu concert as an album launch celebration.

Rumors are flying that she'll have a guest performer with her. This reporter believes it will likely be her new girlfriend, Maya Ryder, but we can't be sure. There have also been rumors that Darren Dawson will be in attendance. If that's true, the ticket holders are even luckier than we thought. One thing is certain: if Darren attends, it's sure to be 'A Night To Remember'.

CHAPTER 36

SAVANNAH

I took a deep breath, looking out from the wings at the stage, trying to calm my racing heart. My pink sparkle bodysuit clung to me like armor as I squeezed Maya's hand tightly. Her mesh black fingerless gloves were a little itchy, but her touch was comforting regardless. She was wearing a matching mesh black crop top with a strappy black bralette under it that I was dying to tear off her. I wasn't sure if she had picked it out to distract me, but I was grateful to her because it was working. My nerves were through the roof, but I kept reminding myself I could do this. We had all prepared for this, and for better or worse, I was about to give everyone a show they would never forget.

This was it. This was what we'd been preparing for, but knowing Darren would probably be here and hearing he actually had the audacity to show up were two different things. I knew Hedge Fund Records would invite him. After all, they were adamant about using my connection with him to boost my popularity. What a joke. If he didn't have pull at the label, he wouldn't be here. I wasn't full of myself, but it was clear that my fame transcended him. If anything, him being here had the potential to be a PR nightmare for me. They were lucky I was emotionally stable enough to see him without it wrecking my show. Although, the more I thought about it, they probably wouldn't care if it wrecked my show. They continually told me that any headlines were good headlines. To them, I was just a performer, a tool they used to make money. They didn't actually care about my wellbeing. It was clearer than ever since they had been using my divorce and emotional turmoil to help sell records.

It disgusted me that they were making money off my pain, but the joke was on them. This would be the last day they made anything off of me. I had a new album to launch and they weren't going to know what hit them.

Taking the stage, the applause was deafening, but my eyes had narrowed onto Darren standing in the wings on the other side of the stage. I hadn't seen him in person since he left, and the arrogant smile made his face look especially punchable today. I took a couple of deep breaths. I had expected him to be sitting front and center, making a spectacle of himself as the supportive, pining, ex-lover. I had no idea what he was doing backstage. If he was trying to throw me off, it worked. My steps faltered for a moment. I turned, looking behind me quickly to where I had just left Maya, wanting a reassuring smile from her, but she was glaring at him. That made me grin. I was glad that for once I wasn't the one on the receiving end of that look.

I crossed the stage to the microphone and took my mark. Waiting for the cheers to die down, I turned to the band, making sure they were ready. Connor's answering grin took away a lot of my nerves. I always performed. It was normal to me, but this show was different. Not only was I going to do a duet with Maya after Hedge Fund Records specifically vetoed it, but I was about to cut ties with them permanently and make my latest album of theirs worthless.

I couldn't wait to share a stage with Maya again. It was exhilarating at Pride and I couldn't wait to experience it again. She was an amazing actress and just as good a singer. She was good at everything she did. Why I had gotten my big break over her was still a mystery to me. I still wasn't sure why they had overlooked her for me in the first place.

Maya and I were going to be performing our duet from my new album, but even if she wasn't on the album, I would have wanted her to perform with me. I wanted to give her the world, and I knew her performing with me again would open more doors for her. Even if she broke my heart again by walking away when this was all over, I still wanted the best for her. She and the rest of her family didn't deserve to be struggling. I knew she wouldn't take money from me, but I still wanted to help her however I could. Even if she chose to walk away, I wanted her to have been better off for having known me.

I took another deep breath. No turning back now. I knew my band and the rest of my team would support me, but I had some concerns about my fans. Although, seeing how they had come out in droves tonight at the last minute, and seeing the overwhelming support I got from them after coming out, I was almost positive they would support me tonight as well. From the mischievous look Darren had on his face, I knew I would need every bit of their support to weather whatever he had planned.

The crowd's cheers had dulled so I grabbed the microphone and was about to welcome everyone when a voice cut me off before I could speak. Hedge Fund Records CEO Mark's voice blared over the speakers. I looked over toward Darren and just then noticed for the first time that Mark was standing right next to him with a hand on his back. Mark stepped out on stage, and behind him came a stagehand with a second microphone.

Had they changed their minds? Were they supporting me singing with Maya, after all?

A glance back to Maya showed her glaring at Mark. *Shit*. She turned on her heel and stormed off. My anxiety rose further. *That's not a good sign..*

"Welcome one and all to the one and only Savannah Hollywood's latest chart-topping album release. Tonight, we really wanted to treat you fans to something truly special. Of course, Savannah's going to perform-" He had to pause for the roaring cheer of the crowds. Even while waiting with bated breath to see what he would say next, I couldn't help feeling a little smug at their response and at them cutting him off.

"But tonight, it's not just about Savannah. Tonight, we have a special guest, or should I say Savannah has a special guest."

I had a sinking feeling about this, but still looked around for Maya. She had to be standing in the wings grinning at me, right? It had to be her, right? But as I glanced around, she was still nowhere to be seen, and to my horror, Darren had taken a couple of steps forward.

No.

I looked at Mark pleadingly and saw my fears confirmed by his shit-eating grin. "I'm sure you all know a little something about Savannah's trail of broken hearts, but no one knows more about that than our surprise guest. Come on out, Darren."

I had to be in hell. Maybe a stage light had fallen and taken me out. It was really the only rational explanation, because this couldn't be happening. But sure enough, he came waltzing out on stage.

What did he think was going to happen? That I was going to rush into his arms and beg him to take me back? For god's sake, he was the one that cheated. Yes, I left him, but he left me no god damn choice, and now he couldn't leave well enough alone. Of course, the second he saw my fans were only interested in him as long as he was with me, now he wanted me back. It would be a frigid day in hell before that happened.

He got to the microphone and looked at me with pleading eyes that made me want to slap him. There was a reason he was an actor, but even I never knew how good he actually was. Two timer. Liar. Manipulator. Cheater. There were a million words I could use to describe him, but actor fit best. I had believed every god damn lie he sold me, believed he loved me, believed he cared, but all he ever cared about was himself.

I took a calming breath and glanced quickly around for any ideas about what to do. Connor looked about ready to get up, but I shook my head subtly. If someone was going to put a stop to this, and I really hoped someone would, it couldn't be Connor. The tabloids would be all over the love triangle they would sell that as, and that was the last thing me or Connor wanted.

Stevie looked ready to move but I shook my head at her, too. Nikki looked frozen in place with worry. I tried to give them a reassuring smile, but I was sure it fell flat. I needed them all to stand their ground, though. My bandmates fighting my battles wouldn't help me and wouldn't look good for any of us. I needed the crowd's support tonight and that might not happen if we made Darren look like a victim.

I looked to the wings hopefully, looking for Maya, or Lexi, or even Clarice, but no one was standing there waiting to rescue me. I took a deep breath, and the beginnings of an idea formed. Maybe I didn't need anyone else, maybe, just maybe, I could rescue myself. Be my own hero. I just had to get that damn microphone away from Darren before he started his monologue, because I was sure I wouldn't come out looking like the good guy if I gave him a piece of my mind after all the bullshit he was about to spew all over the stage.

Unfortunately, I didn't move quick enough; he had already reached the microphone and moved it to his lips. I looked around in confusion when, instead of his voice, a note rang out. A familiar one. A few more notes played, and I gasped when I recognized them. This was Connor's song for Emily.

We had finally finished it a few weeks ago but I couldn't figure out how or why it would be playing now.

I turned around, looking at Connor for an explanation, and froze when I saw how white his face had gotten. I tilted my head at him, mentally asking him if this was him. He slowly shook his head, looking just as confused as I did, if not more. I waited with bated breath, my eyes not leaving Connor's, waiting for him to say just kidding and pull out a microphone, but his face was still ghostly.

A moment later, his voice came in, but I was still watching him and he hadn't said a word. I heard him sing a few more words and saw his face morph from shock into hatred as he glared over my shoulder. It was then that I noticed Darren in my peripheral vision looking at me. I turned and my mouth dropped open, seeing him. He was holding the microphone and mouthing the words. Serenading me, making a mockery of the song Connor and I had worked so hard on for Emily and stealing Connor's voice. He was trying to steal my show.

He started mouthing along that I was his one and only, and the douchebag had the audacity to wink at me. I was going to make him pay for this if it was the last thing I did. I was about to say something when something shiny caught my attention backstage. I glanced over real quick and saw Maya gesturing wildly, when she saw she had my attention. She motioned to Darren and held up a hand motioning for me to wait. That didn't make any sense. If anyone should be behind me tearing him a new one, it should be her. She gestured to someone further backstage that I couldn't see. I watched her turn back to me and saw she was grinning. I was still looking at her questioningly, but she mouthed at me to trust her.

A tall order after everything we'd been through, but I was shocked to find I did trust her.

I glanced back at Darren and saw he was really getting into it now and had to stop myself from gagging. His whole performance was making me sick.

A moment later, I heard a crackle of the microphone and a harsh off-key note that cut off abruptly. From the look on Darren's face, and the lack of vocals, it was easy to tell what happened. Somehow, Maya had cut Connor's recorded vocals and that dying cat sound was Darren. Authentic for the first time in his life.

I couldn't help leaning into my own microphone and saying, "What's wrong? I was really enjoying the show."

He tapped the microphone, and the feedback assaulted my ears. In a panic, he looked at Mark who was standing off stage and looked just as alarmed. "I think we're experiencing some technical difficulties," Darren said apologetically to the crowd.

Oh no, he didn't. He wasn't getting off that easily.

"Mine works just fine," I said into it, demonstrating, "And it sounded just now like yours does, too. I think Darren's feeling a little shy." I frowned dramatically and turned to the crowd. "What do we say, guys, do you want to hear him sing?"

They started to cheer, and I watched him expectantly. He stood there like a deer in headlights and I basked in his discomfort for a moment before adding the cherry on top, saying, "Sing to me, Darren."

He tried to pick up where he left off, but the sound that came out of the microphone sounded more like two cats fighting in an alley than it did singing. I just grinned. He continued his caterwauling for another moment before the boos started and rose loud enough to drown him out, thank goodness.

After a moment of him watching in disbelief, he looked at me pleadingly. I would have felt bad if I didn't know the performance was still for the cameras, ever the actor.

I picked up my microphone, and a hush fell over the crowd. He looked relieved, but I was about to change that.

"You want to know what I really think about you? How about the truth? The only thing honest about you is that god awful singing voice we all just heard. You want real? You broke my heart into a million pieces and left me bleeding, and now that I've pieced myself back together bit by bit and rose from the ashes of the bridge you burnt, now you come crawling back. Now that my fans abandoned you in droves, now that you see they were only coming to your movies for me, now you want me back? Well, it's too late. You left me and I had to learn how to be okay on my own. I picked myself up and healed myself. You had no part in that and you won't have a part in my life anymore. I'm done, Dare. Why don't you crawl back to whoever let you into their bed this week and leave me alone?"

"Is this about that whore you're seeing? Megan? Molly? Whatever the hell her name is? I mean god," he said, looking at the crowd, "you guys can't honestly buy that. From the way she squeals when I fuck her, there's no way she's a lesbian."

The collective gasps of the crowd almost drowned out my response, almost. "Her name's Maya, and you should hear the noises I make for her."

Maya, as if on cue, came sauntering out to the screaming crowd, but even the roar of the crowd couldn't drown out her "That's my girl." She was grinning ear to ear, making my heart do a backflip. "And she's bisexual, not a lesbian," she added.

I felt it right then and there, the point of no return in my heart. I was falling in love with this brilliant, beautiful, firecracker of a woman. The relationship might be fake, but there was nothing fake about my feelings.

I couldn't help adding, "She's right. I like men, too, just not you."

Maya stepped to my side and handed me a folder. I looked down at it quickly, not understanding. My face broke from confusion into a grin when I spotted Lexi's legal letterhead popping out of the folder. The divorce papers I had been trying, with no luck, to serve him.

"Actually, on second thought, I do have something you can do for me." He looked at me hopefully for a moment before I stepped forward, saying sweetly, "I could use an autograph."

I shoved the folder into his hands and saw him look at it with confusion, opening the folder and taking in the papers. Anger flashed over his face. I stepped back to Maya and said into the microphone, "You've been served. See you in court."

The applause drowned out whatever response he had. I watched him tapping on his mic, but nothing happened. He glared at me, and I was grateful the cameras were zoomed in enough to catch it. I glanced up and saw his face magnified on the screens behind us and on either side of the stage. The audience quieted for a moment before the "boos" started. I heard some people yelling "get off the stage" and I couldn't keep the grin off my face. He stomped his foot and threw down the microphone, turning and storming off the stage to the crowd's cheering.

He barreled past Mark, who was waiting in the wings and immediately turned and quickly followed him. *Good riddance.*

It was time to take back the spotlight.

"Now that that's taken care of. I have a bit of news for you all. Darren and I aren't the only ones breaking up tonight."

The crowd gasped, and I felt Maya stiffen next to me. Shit, that came out wrong.

"Tonight, Hedge Fund Records and I are calling it quits, too."

Maya relaxed against me and I couldn't believe that for a minute she actually thought I was going to end things with her right here and now. Never mind that I was the further I had ever been from wanting to end things. Even if I had wanted to, I would never be cruel enough to do it on a stage in front of my fans. I squeezed her hand, hoping to reassure her, and smiled when she squeezed back.

"It wasn't easy to break things off with them, but I knew it needed to be done. They weren't supportive of my new life direction," I said, holding up Maya's hand. The crowd booed and I heard a few calls of "Fuck Hedge Fund" "Screw those homophobes" and I couldn't help smiling.

"They told me to dull myself down. They would have preferred me to be a little less rainbow."

The crowd roared louder at that, anger coursing through them. It touched me to know how much they all cared. It was overwhelming.

I blinked back the tears in my eyes and continued, "So you know what I told them?"

The crowd roared in anticipation.

"I told them that storms make rainbows and I was prepared to weather this one."

They screamed louder at that and I grinned. "And that's not all. I was torn with how to handle my latest album, since I obviously didn't want to give another dollar to someone who didn't support me and my people. I wouldn't want any of you to have to support them just to listen to my music, so you know what I did?"

I waited for the cheers to die down before saying, "They owned the recordings, but they don't own my songs. They don't own me. So, I present to you," I waved my hands to the giant screen behind me as the rainbow phoenix emblem came up, "Rising From the Ashes: The Rainbow Edition."

The crowd went wild at that and I was grinning so hard it hurt.

"It has all the same songs as the original album, but half the proceeds are going directly to LGBTQ+ charities and the other half are going to a foundation I developed for queer artists to help them make it in the industry."

The crowd cheered louder. I had to cut through the noise to add, "For those of you that already bought Hedge Fund Records' version, on my website there's a form; upload a picture of your receipt and we'll send you a digital version of the new album for free. For anyone who hasn't bought the album yet, you won't want to miss the Rainbow Edition. Not only is it beautiful..." I gestured to the screen as photos of the rainbow CD and vinyl came up. The crowd's approval was deafening. "...there's also three new tracks and new features on the old songs."

The screen ran through the names of the featuring artists, leaving Maya's name for last.

"Now that you all know, who wants to hear the song me and my girlfriend cooked up for you?"

I looked at her and said, "Why don't you help me out, love?"

The intensity of the cheers warmed my heart and my cheeks. The gasps came a moment later when I noticed Connor stand up out of the corner of my eye. I started laughing and saw Maya was, too.

"He's just playing. Come on, sit down. Tonight's my night," I told him playfully.

The crowd laughed at that, harder when he said into his mic, "So different from every other night."

I rolled my eyes and chuckled before turning back to the crowd. "In case anyone missed it, this is Maya, my girlfriend, and as I'm sure you remember from Hollywood High, she has a damn good voice. Do you want to hear her sing?"

The audience went wild.

I grinned at her, and just like we rehearsed, asked, "What do you say, love? You think you're up for it?"

She grinned back and the way her eyes lit up, I could tell the adrenaline was hitting her. "Do you think you can handle me, Hollywood?" she asked, smirking.

My face was red now, I felt flushed, and felt the heat rush to my core. I was finding I didn't mind so much when she called me that anymore. From her smirk, she knew exactly what she was doing to me.

The audience went wild, and right on cue, the band took up the beat.

CHAPTER 37

MAYA

Hearing Sav belt out notes onstage was a religious experience and I would crawl across broken glass to hear it. Her voice gave me full body chills. When my voice mixed with hers, the result was electric. Our voices fit together, elevating the song. The words were coated in passion and I meant every one of them. Singing with her did something to me, and I could see it in her eyes that this was affecting her the same way.

We had rehearsed enough that I was sure I could do this in my sleep, thankfully. I hadn't expected to feel so distracted by her. I was still running over her words in my head. She had just admitted to the world that we've been intimate and that I'm good in bed. It was the last thing I expected from her, and god I couldn't wait to make her moan again, to make her scream my name.

As much as I wanted to be with her, it wasn't just that. Yes, she was captivating, but singing with her brought up more feelings than I expected. Singing a love song with her was almost too much to handle. From the way she was undressing me with her eyes, it seemed like she felt the same.

Thankfully, she could work a crowd in her sleep and didn't falter. When she brushed against me, I felt my whole body respond. When she was singing just to me, everyone else ceased to exist. The reason we were on stage together in the first place ceased to exist. Even the song itself didn't matter. This whole performance was just musical foreplay, and I was running through mental images of where and how I was going to take her the second I could get her alone. There must be a dressing room, or trailer, or even a damned storage closet that I could get her alone in. I needed her badly. The where didn't matter, but I needed her screaming my name in that angelic voice of hers.

It was going to be a long show, and it was going to kill me waiting for her. Thankfully, I knew she had an outfit change during her next song and I would be waiting for her. Poor Connor was going to have to extend his drum solo longer than he planned, because her "quick change" wasn't going to be quick if I had anything to say about it.

SAVANNAH HOLLYWOOD STARTS A NEW CHAPTER

In a jaw dropping turn of events last night, Savannah Holly-wood publicly turned down her soon-to-be ex-husband who stole onto stage at her album release and begged for her back. He tried to serenade her, but it appeared a cat got his tongue when the music he was lip-syncing to was cut. Who knew Darren Dawson could do such a realistic impression of a dying cat? He must be a far better actor than we've been giving him credit for.

Savannah laid into him and after some homophobic com-ments, she served him with their divorce papers and he ran offstage. Surprisingly, that wasn't the most shocking part of the evening. Savannah had another surprise up her sleeve.

She announced she parted ways with Hedge Fund Records, a ballsy move at a concert held for her album re-lease with them. You're probably wondering why and what this means for her album and why she left. Well, she didn't leave us wondering. She told the crowd she was parting with Hedge Fund Records since they didn't support her new lifestyle. While she didn't specifically say it was because of her bisexuality, she did hold up her girlfriend, Maya Ryder's hand when she referenced her new lifestyle. It doesn't take a genius to figure out her label wasn't supportive of her sexuality.

Instead of taking that lying down, she stood up for herself and reclaimed her album in a surprising way. She rerecorded and released a different version of the new album called "Rising From The Ashes: The Rainbow Edition." The Rainbow Edition has all the same songs as the original but with new features from other queer artists, including a special feature from her girlfriend, Maya Ryder. Her fans have been quick to support and snatch up the new album, calling it the queer version, the better and gayer version.

If you're asking yourself why you should bother buying another album if you already bought the first one, her team has a form on their website and with proof of purchase of the first one, they send you a free digital version of the album. In order to get the physical version, which is a beautiful rainbow color, you'll need to repurchase it, but half the proceeds go to LGBTQ+ charities and the other half to a new foundation she started to help other queer artists make it in the industry.

We applaud Savannah for standing her ground and standing up for herself and the LGBTQ+ community and for blessing us with the queer fierceness on the Rainbow Edition of her album. The straight version Hedge Fund Records is selling doesn't hold a candle to how much the Rainbow Editions slays.

CHAPTER 38

SAVANNAH

When Lexi got a call that Darren was going to be appearing on Celebs Spill All with Mark from Hedge Fund Records to talk about my latest album and spill on my split with him and Hedge Fund Records, we knew what to do. The audio recording of my meeting with them was ready to go as well as an emotional video confession I did. For once everything was going right and I couldn't wait to see his face. I was lucky he chose a show whose host was partial to me and gave us the warning. She invited me to the studio, but I decided against it. I had seen enough of him at my concert and knew I would be forced to see a lot more of him in divorce court. I didn't need to see him again so soon, but I did invite the band, Lexi, Clarice, and Miss Lucy Fur all over to my screening room to watch him and my old record label get more of their just desserts.

We settled in with popcorn and watched on the drama play out on my theatre screen.

Host: Give a warm welcome to Darren Dawson, famous actor and soon to be ex-husband of famous popstar Savannah Hollywood and to Mark Nicholson, the CEO of Hedge Fund Records.

The audience cheered as Darren and Mark joined the Host on stage and both took seats on the couch.

Darren: Thank you so much for having us. It's been an emotional week and to be honest I really wasn't sure if I wanted to come on here, but when I heard from Mark how Savannah had ended things spitefully with Hedge Fund Records, I knew he needed my support.

Mark: I didn't even want to come out. I figured we were under enough of a spotlight and didn't need the extra attention.

Mark smiled sheepishly.

Mark: But Darren here, good friend that his is, convinced me that people deserve to know the truth

Darren: I'm proud of you, buddy. It takes a real man to open up to the public about how he's feeling and I for one am proud of you for being here.

Darren turned to the crowd.

Darren: You're all proud of him. too, aren't you?

The crowd applauded him.

Host: We are truly grateful you both came on the show. So, getting to the elephant, or should we say popstar royalty in the room, you said you have something to share about Savannah?

Darren nodded solemnly.

Darren: We do. Firstly, I want to make it clear I have nothing but respect for the LGBTQ+ community.

Mark: As do I.

Darren: Unfortunately, I don't have respect for Savannah anymore. In addition to ripping off her own record and taking food out of the mouths of hundreds of kids of Hegde Fund Records employees, she's been lying to you all. She's no more a part of the LGBTQ+ community than I am.

The audience gasped and some boos could be heard.

Mark: It pains us to tell you, but it's the truth. Her and Maya's relationship has been fake since day one. She hired her to pose as her girlfriend to get good press and make you all stop paying attention to the truths Darren was sharing about her.

Darren: I think she thought it would make me jealous, and I hope you don't think less of me when I say it did a little bit. Especially when I bared my heart to her on stage and she couldn't have kicked me out faster. After she flaunted her relationship in front of me, Mark was a true friend and broke his confidentially agreement to let me know it was fake.

Host: Are you saying Savannah's not actually bisexual? That she's lying about her sexuality?

Mark: There's nothing bisexual about her. She's a bitter woman who's clearly still in love with Darren and doing this for attention.

Darren shot Mark a brief look that the camera caught. Mark stopped talking.

Darren: I think what Mark means to say is that we know sexuality is complicated, but it's not a normal thing to hire someone to pretend to date you. If she were actually bisexual, she could have had her pick of women. There was no need to hire one, and she wouldn't have unless she had something to hide. She's fake and not actually bisexual and we thought you all deserved to know the truth, especially now that she's selling queer albums and trying to make money off of the LGBTQ+ community.

People booed at that, before the Host hushed them.

Host: Those certainly are some big accusations.

Darren's carefully curated sad little smile faltered for a moment. His eyes widened and he looked at Mark, who looked much the same.

Host: Do you have any evidence to back them up?

Darren: What evidence would you need that someone is straight? It's like asking someone to prove they're queer, which we all certainly know shouldn't be done.

Host: Of course not, of course, but saying she hired a girlfriend to parade around as a bisexual is a big accusation. Do either of you have proof that Maya was hired? A contract perhaps? Evidence money was exchanged? Anything?

Darren and Mark both visibly paled at this.

Mark: I haven't seen the contract myself, but as Savannah's record label at the time, she made Hedge Fund Records aware of her plan.

Host: So, she told you that she was pretending to be bisexual in order to get good publicity?

Mark swallowed hard.

Mark: Not in so many words, but she did say she was hiring a fake girlfriend and why else would she if not to try to lie to the world about being bisexual.

Host turned to the audience.

Host: Let me get this straight. What I'm hearing is these men are making baseless accusations about a queer woman who isn't here to defend herself. What do we think of that, friends?

The boos were deafening.

Host: Lucky for everyone, Savannah is able to weigh in.

Darren and Mark were now ghostly shades of white as the crowd roared.

Host: Unfortunately, she couldn't be here, but she did send in an illuminating little video. Gentlemen, if you'll turn your attention to the scene behind you, we can see what she has to say for herself.

Behind Darren and Mark, Savannah's face popped up on the big screen. She was front and center with Maya Ryder off to the right. Maya had a supportive hand on Savannah's shoulder.

Savannah: Thank you so much for letting me tell my side of the story. I'm sure Hedge Fund Records had some tales to tell and I'd like to tell you all my story. My contract with Hedge Fund Records ended with my last album Rising From the Ashes. Everyone knows I then chose to release my own version and I want to thank you all from the bottom of my heart for supporting it, but it's time you all know why I made the decision I did. The CEO of Hedge Fund Records is best friends with Darren, my soon to be ex-husband, and to say my relationship with Mark and the label has been strained since then is an understatement. Had that been the only problem, I would have given them my last album and quietly moved on, but they wouldn't let me part on good terms. When it became clear to Hedge Fund Records I had no intent of re-signing with them, they became openly hostile toward me. Again, I dealt with it, but things came to a head after I came out as bisexual. I was called into a meeting with Hedge Fund Records CEO Mark Nicholson who berated me for my sexuality and told me that for my career I needed to take back my husband. Up until that point, I had been treated with what I thought was hostility, but that was nothing compared to this. The Hedge Fund Records CEO then told me that if I didn't sign the contract, they would tell everyone that I wasn't actually bisexual and that I was paying my girlfriend to be with me. I broke down and was almost bullied into signing their contract. I might have if it wasn't for my wonderful girlfriend Maya and the unwavering love and support from my team who are like a family to me. My newest album Rising From the Ashes: The Rainbow Edition is my way of reclaiming my voice from the cishet men who would rather I stay silent, and I thank you all for supporting me.

Darren and Mark were just barely containing their anger.

Host: I know I said big accusations shouldn't be said without proof, but Savannah didn't come without receipts.

Darren: This is ridiculous! You're not really going to believe Savannah, are you? She's just trying to ruin me and my friends!

Host: If you'll turn your ears to the screen, this audio clip will be most informative.

Savannah

I turned down the volume as the audio clip was played. Everyone with me had already heard it anyway and I didn't want to relive it.

Besides, everyone was talking all at once anyway, so no one would have been able to hear it.

Nikki was in Stevie's arms. Connor was mimicking Darren's startled expression, making Lexi burst out in laughter. Miss Lucy was calling Darren and Hedge

Fund Records every cuss word in the book, and inventing some creative new ones. Clarice was sitting next to her, nodding vigorously.

Maya folded me into her arms and said softly to me, "I'm so proud of you."

I grinned, loving the feeling of belonging and happiness that was washing over me. If all it took was hitting rock bottom and my marriage falling apart for the pieces of my life to fall together, I would do it a million times over. All the pain was worth it to be surrounded by all the love I was feeling now.

They were all here for me, to support me, and had all gone out of their way over the past few weeks to make sure I knew I was cared for. I couldn't thank them enough and was so glad they were all here. Folded into Maya's arms, surrounded by the family I had made for myself, I wanted to bask in the moment forever. I knew it wouldn't last forever, but tried to push the thoughts of Maya's contract ending soon out of my mind. With how far we had come, even if she didn't actually want to be with me, she would still have to stay in my life. There was no way she wouldn't want anything to do with me after everything we had been through together. At least I tried to tell myself that.

CHAPTER 39

MAYA

Sav and I had been keeping our distance the past week. We were both busy, her with the new album and me with evaluating potential new jobs. The contract was ending soon and for once, my email was littered with offers. I was ecstatic, but it was hard to ignore the pain at the thought of having to leave Sav. I kept thinking that the next day we would talk about it, but she was so busy and I didn't want to be the one to bring it up. She knew the situation we were in and if she hadn't said anything yet, it must be because she was okay with things ending.

I hated that I had been stupid enough to fall for her. I had known it was a bad idea, and now here I was careening toward our end, the planned end I knew was coming, and I couldn't stop thinking about her. I tried to tell myself it was just about her lips, about her tongue, about the taste of her. Tried to convince myself I wasn't thinking about her smile that lit up a room, her eyes that made my heart stop, her laugh that I would do anything to hear. I couldn't be thinking that way, so if my heart quickened whenever I saw her, I did my best to tell my brain that it was nothing but hormones and sexual tension. Produced by Sav's mesmerizing hips and thighs, certainly not by my own traitorous heart.

I wasn't falling, hadn't fallen. I couldn't have, since it was doomed from the start. We were always headed toward the monumental break up that was coming. I had wanted that badly, had savored the thought of finally getting to publicly give her her just desserts, but now it felt surprisingly unsatisfying.

It crossed my mind for a few shining moments that I didn't have to do this if I didn't want to. I could stay the course and see how things went, keep squeezing every moment from her she would give me. I could just not do it, to hell with the consequences. I could make her admit how she actually felt for once. I didn't have to make this easy for her. If she wanted out, I could make her be the one to do it. After all, why would I make her life easier?

I didn't have to do this, and if I was being honest with myself, really, truly honest, I didn't want to. I didn't want whatever weird thing I had with Sav to end. The irony of being contractually obligated to publicly break her heart, a prospect I was ecstatic about when I first saw it was her a couple of months ago, wasn't lost on me.

As nice as the fantasy was, I knew this was the end. I wasn't the one with a hefty legal team on my side; I had to stay the course. If I didn't, Elite could and would sue me within an inch of my life. Sav was the only one with the power to stop this, and I knew better than to trust her to be looking out for my best interest. I had gotten too close to her. I was the worst kind of fool for letting her have access to my heart again. I only hoped this time I could make it out with some of my dignity intact.

With a sigh, I picked up my favorite lipstick and painted my lips a deep purple. If this ship was going down, I was going to look damned good while it did.

CHAPTER 40

SAVANNAH

As I was being shuffled between the hair and makeup team, it occurred to me that this was the first time in a long time that I was getting ready without Maya. Of course, I offered to have my team take care of her, too, but she refused. It was probably for the best; I was going to have to get used to getting ready without her. Might as well start now. But I couldn't ignore the ache in my heart when I saw a shade of purple that reminded me of her favorite lipstick, which made me think of her very kissable lips.

I slumped in my chair with a groan, which was when Lexi came waltzing in. I saw her arch a brow at me before moving around my hair stylist and settling into the chair next to me. She grabbed my hand and squeezed.

"I'm so proud of you. Hang in there, love, you've just got to get through tonight and then you're home free."

Correction, I thought, *Maya just has to get through tonight and then she's home free. I don't think I'd ever consider myself free again with the vice grip she has on my heart. My stupid, fragile, breaking heart.*

I felt like I did back all those years ago, like her walking away was for the best, but might kill me in the process. That her staying was sure to ruin me, but her leaving would break me just the same. I was a ruined woman one way or the other. The only choice I had left was picking my poison.

I looked at Lexi and she startled at the expression on my face. I should have been masking my feelings better, but it was Lexi and I couldn't bring myself to care.

She leaned closer, really looking at me, and said, "I thought you'd be relieved this was almost over. I know you hate the lies."

I sighed. "You're not wrong, but somewhere along the line, it stopped feeling as much like a lie."

Her eyes widened. "Are you saying what I think you're saying?"

I wasn't sure I was capable of saying the words out loud, so I just nodded.

"Shit."

"You can say that again."

"I'm guessing she doesn't feel the same?"

I swallowed over the lump in my throat and shook my head. "Of course she doesn't."

At that, she narrowed her eyes at me. "The hell do you mean 'of course she doesn't'?" she asked, emphasizing my own words with dramatic air quotes.

"She hates me, or hated me, or maybe still does. I really don't know. The whole act has been confusing as hell. One minute she's acting like she's as into this as I am, and the next she pulls away and gets distant again. I don't know what she wants, but I know it can't be me. She's made that much clear. The sex is just clouding my brain, that has to be all this is-"

"THE WHAT IS WHAT?!" Lexi screeched at a volume that I was sure they could hear her in outer space.

"Shhh!" I told her quickly, wincing at my startled hair stylist. She shot Lexi a warning look that would have sent anyone else running, but Lexi just said, "Sorry, I'll keep it down."

She nodded and got back to work. Lexi leaned closer to me. "So, when were you going to tell me?"

I shrugged. "You knew how close we've been lately."

Now she glared at me. "Cut the shit. I know how close you were having to act like you were. I thought you were just a good actress."

I looked at her incredulously. "I'm not that good."

She rolled her eyes. "You're damned good and you know it. Quit fishing for compliments and give me the details on what the hell has been going on with you."

"It's not that big a deal. I was just doing what I was supposed to."

She blinked at me, waiting. When I didn't say more, she threw her hands up in exasperation.

"I told you you had to make it look real, but come on! How long has something been going on?"

"It's really not that big of a deal." I hoped that sounded more convincing to her than it felt to me, but from the way her face didn't change, I knew it hadn't.

"As your one-woman business team, I have to be looped in. This could have been a walking PR nightmare if you weren't careful."

I gawked at her. "You literally signed me up for this. Don't have so little faith in your abilities. If you signed off on it, there's no way it could be a disaster."

She laughed at that. "Okay fine, new tactic; as your best friend, you should have told me. I thought there was something between you two, but figured I was imagining things cause you would've told me if something happened."

The guilt weighed on me. She was right, I should've told her. I had wanted to, but couldn't find the right time or the right words. I didn't even really know what was going on with us, never mind how to explain it to her.

I finally settled on saying, "I just really didn't think it mattered. We have a scheduled break up, and it's not like either of us have talked about how we're feeling. We have a contractual end date," I looked at her pointedly, adding, "of today actually, so it doesn't do me any good to get hung up on my feelings that don't matter."

"Of course they matter! They matter to me and if she's cruel enough that they don't matter to her, I'll make damn sure she doesn't work in this industry again."

"Lex, it's not like that." I said, rolling my eyes. "I just don't think she cares about me how I care about her. I didn't realize until she came waltzing back into my life just how much I missed her. The idea of her walking away again hurts, but that's her right. You can't make her jobless because she doesn't want to be with me."

She huffed. "I'm damn sure I could." I leveled her with a look that made her laugh before saying, "Fine. Fine. I won't do shit unless you ask me to, but I still say blacklisting her from the business if she breaks your heart is fair game."

"Her having issues in the industry is the last thing I want. That's what ended our friendship the first go round."

She took my hand again and squeezed. "I promise I won't interfere, but I really think you should tell her how you feel."

"I don't even really know how I feel."

She gave me a pointed look. "But you know there are feelings."

"Complicated, messy ones I can't name."

"Complicated, messy feelings that you're scared of but familiar with nonetheless. No one blames you for being scared of falling for someone again, but for what it's worth, I don't think she's anything like Darren."

I sighed. "I can't trust her, though. She's walked away from me once. She's going to do it again."

"You're right."

I startled, whipping my head in her direction and having to apologize to my hair stylist. I had never been more grateful for the iron clad NDAs Lexi made everyone who worked with me sign. I watched Lexi, waiting for her to explain herself. I had been expecting her to console me or tell me I was wrong, not agree with me.

"You're damn right she's going to walk away if you don't stop her. She is contractually obligated to walk away and never look back if you don't stop her. So, you have to decide, and quickly. If you want her in your life, you have to say something."

"That's not fair. I have no idea how she feels, but if she doesn't want to walk away, she doesn't have to."

"You might not have thoroughly read her contract, but I did, and there's no wiggle room in it for her. She has to break up with you tonight, never talk about anything private that passed between the two of you, and never initiate contact with you again unless explicitly approved by you."

"Shit."

"Yeah, I was impressed. Whoever drafted those knew what they were doing. Even I couldn't find a loophole when I was approving the paperwork."

Shit, so it really was all on me. But how the hell could I tell her how I feel when I don't have the first clue how she feels?

"So, what you're saying is there's no way she's able to stick around."

"No, not unless you ask her to."

"I can't."

"Correction, you're not going to, but you should. You're perfectly capable. What's the worst that can happen?"

"Absolute worst? She laughs in my face about how gullible I am, says she's always been a better actress than me, and says other cruel things like how she'd never actually be caught dead with me, or that she could never trust me again, or something equally terrible like that."

"Do you really think she would do that?"

"I'm scared."

"I know. Falling is always scary, but the right person is there to catch you. I know Darren let you fall on your face, but it's not always like that. It's not supposed to be like that, but you'll never know how she feels if you don't give her a chance to tell you."

"I guess."

"Promise you'll think about it."

I nodded. "I promise." I could do that much. Even if I didn't want to, I was sure I wouldn't be able to think about anything else today, anyway.

When I slid into the backseat of the limo to join Maya, it was bittersweet seeing her. She was dressed to kill in a deep purple dress that draped off her shoulders. It was much more revealing than what she would normally wear, making it clear it was Miss Lucy's one last outfit for her. The scowl on her face was almost laughable, or it would have been if I wasn't worried that the scowl was for me and not the outfit.

"At least it matches your favorite lipstick," I said with a small, apologetic smile. After all, it was my fault she was in this mess in the first place.

She looked startled for a moment before grinning. "I shouldn't be surprised you stare at my lips enough to know it's my favorite."

My cheeks burned red, but I stammered out the obvious, "You look beautiful."

She smirked at that. "I look like exactly who I'm supposed to be tonight."

I looked at her, confused.

After a moment, she elaborated, "A heartbreaker."

My heart sank when she gave me a rueful smile. Now would be a good time to say something. It felt like it was now or never, but her smile stilled my tongue. She seemed like she wanted this. The woman sitting across from me was a far cry from the woman who had been sharing my bed and I didn't know how to reach her. I reached out my hand toward her, but she didn't grasp mine, didn't move. I felt my breath quicken in my lungs and my chest tighten. I felt my heart aching. It was now or never. I didn't want to lose her again, and if I didn't say anything, I would.

"My-"

"Don't," was all she said.

Message received.

CHAPTER 41

MAYA

The party was in full swing by the time we got there, and I was grateful for the distraction. I looked around, surveying the chaos that was the mansion party we were at. It was for some celebrity or another who had won some sort of award. I couldn't remember, nor did I really care. Inside the fenced in area, we were led to was a giant pool with no one in it. There were women in gowns and men in tuxes milling about. The music was loud and there was a dance floor closer to the mansion set up on the sprawling lawn. The mansion itself was huge with two large twin staircases leading to a balcony that entered the home. I scanned the space again and found what I was looking for in the back corner and took off. The bar. I beelined for it, not checking to see if she was following me. It didn't matter. After tonight she wouldn't be around, anyway.

After tonight I would get my life back, things would go back to normal. Well, I amended, hopefully better than normal with the potential jobs I had lined up. Yes, the money from Elite was more than enough to have me, Gram, Leslie, and Kat all set up for quite a while, but I wanted more than that. I wanted stability. I wanted security.

Fuck it, if I was being actually honest with myself, I wanted fame. I wanted to be a household name like Savannah was. I wanted to matter.

Maybe if I mattered enough, she would regret losing me. I downed the glass that was put in front of me, not caring what it was, just needing to feel the burn as it traveled down my throat, needing to feel numb. I couldn't even stand to look at her. I couldn't stand seeing the pity in her eyes.

Earlier, when she had been trying to let me down easy, when she casually used my nickname like my heart wasn't breaking at the idea of not having her in my life, it was too much. I didn't want to hear anything she had to say anymore. She was leaving, and I'd be damned if I showed I cared.

Chapter 42

Savannah

Maya had been avoiding me since we entered the party, and from the way she was hitting the bar, she seemed to think tonight was something to celebrate. I just felt nauseous. I was surrounded by people, but not a single person I was interested in being around. Lexi had offered to come of course, but I thought that would make it harder to do what needed to be done. Besides, I didn't really know what Maya was going to say, and I didn't want Lexi around if things got ugly, and with the way Maya was acting, it seemed like they might.

I checked my phone as discreetly as I could. It was 10:55. I sucked in a breath. Only five more minutes until we got this over with and I could get my life back. I looked around, looking for a good spot. We wanted to be overheard, but not obvious. We needed to put on a show.

There was a balcony overlooking the space that looked perfect. It gave the air of being secluded while still making sure our voices would travel enough to be heard. I moved to the stairs but was stopped on the first stair by a hand on my shoulder. I turned around, expecting it to be Maya, but was surprised to see not her purple and black hair, but a head of bouncing red curls. That was as much as I saw before she pulled me into her arms. Amber.

It had been years since we had last seen each other, but I was beyond excited to see her.

"What are you doing here?" I asked eagerly.

"Are you kidding? The second I heard Savannah Hollywood was gonna be here, I came running. Girl, I missed you like crazy."

I grinned, feeling genuinely happy for the first time all day. Amber and I got really close after Maya and I had our falling out years ago, but I hadn't seen her since she opened for one of my tours a couple of years ago. She and I had been trying to make our schedules work, but her career had blown up over the past year and we hadn't been able to find the time to see each other. When we pulled apart, I saw her grin mirrored mine.

She looked me up and down before whispering conspiratorially, "Plus, you've been radio silent for the last few weeks, so I had to track you down."

I laughed at that. Clarice still hadn't been letting us access much in the way of social media, so I'm sure Amber wasn't the only one who felt my absence, but I was touched she noticed. "I'm so happy you're here."

"If you thought anything would keep me away from you and the tea I'm going to need you to spill, you're crazier than I thought."

"Tea?"

"Only the story of the century! You and Maya? What the hell happened there? I thought you two hated each other."

This was the last thing I wanted to talk about right now. It felt like my secrets were creeping up on me. I was keeping them in as best I could, but they were threatening to erupt from me. I hated the lying, especially to those close to me.

"It's a long story."

"And we have all night."

There wasn't any way I was getting out of this. I knew from experience Amber would keep pushing until I relented, so with a sigh, I started to tell her the story. Unfortunately, it was the same lie of a cover story we were pedaling to everyone else. That was one good thing about tonight, at least. After tonight, the lie would be over.

CHAPTER 43

MAYA

I downed another drink and checked my phone. I had seen her heading to the balcony a while ago. I was sure she was coming here so I had moved through the crowd to meet her, but where the hell was she? She was supposed to have been here 10 minutes ago. I rolled my eyes, getting more annoyed by the second. I was sick of waiting. She wasn't even respectful enough to be on time for our breakup.

A waiter found his way up to me and gave me a glass of champagne. When I looked at him questioningly, he shrugged and said, "Seemed to me like the most beautiful girl at the party deserved a drink."

He was handsome in the traditional sense, but he should have known he did nothing for me. Flattery from men like him, from men in general, did nothing for me. It was a struggle to keep the disdain from my face.

I needed to find Savannah and get this shit over with. The sooner we did it, the sooner I could go home, really home. The thought was both exciting and depressing. I would be on my own again. Sav wouldn't be there every day. I wouldn't be staying in someone else's home. I would be back in my own space, but something told me my one bedroom apartment with my sturdy queen-sized bed was going to feel lonely without someone to share it with. It had been nice to not spend all my nights alone. But I had done it before, and I could and would do it again.

I looked around and spotted her toward the bottom of the stairs, and annoyance prickled until I saw who she was with. Amber. The redheaded singer Savannah replaced me with all those years ago, and now she had her arm on *my* girlfriend. I didn't have to be close to see the way she was looking at Savannah, and I was halfway down the stairs before I knew what I was doing.

Holding the champagne glass in a death grip, my other hand balled into a fist as I closed the distance. How fucking dare she. How dare she stand me up to talk to the woman she replaced me with all those years ago.

Tears were prickling behind my eyes, but I pushed past them, focusing on my anger.

"What the fuck, Amber? Get your hands off *my girlfriend.*"

I heard Savannah gasp, but my narrowed eyes were focused on Amber. I readied myself for whatever was going to happen next, but saw red when Savannah had the nerve to step protectively in front of Amber.

"My," she said slowly, the warning implied. Amber still had her hand on Sav's shoulder. It was all I could see, and with Savannah defending her, it enraged me.

"What, Hollywood?" I said, injecting venom into my voice. I saw the hurt flash in her eyes for a moment and relished in it. It had been a while since I called her that, and we both knew it, but I was done playing nice. Once again, she was proving why I couldn't trust her. That I would never be a priority to her. She couldn't even be on time for our breakup. "Upset you can't control me like everyone else in your life? Well, surprise, I'm not on your payroll, so you can't order me around. Besides, you couldn't afford me."

I was surprised when the hurt was just as quickly replaced by anger. "What the hell are you talking about? The only thing I'm trying to make you do is control your tone." She stepped closer and said lower, "There's people watching."

I didn't lower my tone. In fact, I got louder. "You think I give a fuck about who can hear me? Fuck that. The whole world should know what a goddamn hypocrite you are. You clearly don't give a shit about me and I'm sick of trying to convince myself otherwise. You're clearly the same conniving, scheming liar of a girl you were back at Hollywood High."

Amber tried to step around Savannah, but Sav pushed her back. I was pleased to see she wasn't gentle about it.

"You're wrong about me," she said, her voice wavering. I could see her control slipping and I wanted to keep pushing. I couldn't stop myself. If this ship was going down in flames, I wouldn't be the only one to crash and burn.

"The only thing I was wrong about was thinking I could trust you, thinking for a second that you cared about me enough to not only be looking out for yourself."

"Of course I care about you, you idiot. I'm falling in love with you."

I paled. That wasn't part of the plan. None of this was part of the plan, but that certainly wasn't. Even when she was underneath me, she had never said anything even remotely close to that.

"If you weren't so goddamned infuriating all the time, I would have told you sooner. I'm not perfect, My. I don't pretend to be. I'm the first to admit my faults, but you're not being fair. You hurt me back then, too. You aren't innocent in this."

I was reeling from the emotional whiplash her words were giving me. She was wrong. She was the one who caused the rift between us. She wrecked us all those years ago, and I'd be damned if I let her be the one to have the last word again this time.

I took a calming breath and managed to not scream in frustration. I needed to get out of here, and quickly. I had thought about this moment for weeks, savored the fantasies of leaving Hollywood's It Girl humiliated, of breaking her heart, but now that I was here, it wasn't nearly as satisfying as I thought and I was mortified to feel an echoing pain in my own heart. I just wanted this over with. I had wasted too much energy on her already. I had said what needed to be said, what I should have said a long time ago, and now I just felt numb.

"It's over," was all I cared enough to say before turning on my heel and walking away from her for the last time. Forever.

CHAPTER 44

SAVANNAH

I stood there, stunned, staring after her retreating form. *What the hell was that?* It wasn't that we had planned tonight out, but that was the last way I imagined it going. It had hurt more than I thought it would, watching her walk away without so much as a backward glance.

I startled, feeling a hand on my shoulder. Amber. I had forgotten she was there and that I was unfortunate enough for her to have witnessed that. I didn't care about anyone else here, had made sure everyone I cared about steered clear and didn't have to see me like this, but Amber was the last person I expected to be here.

When I met her eye and saw the look of concern on her face, my heart ached even more than it already did.

"Is there anything I can do?" she asked quietly. "I'm so sorry if I caused you any trouble."

The moment the words left her mouth, a switch flipped in me, sending all my sadness and despair careening over into anger.

Maya had some fucking audacity using Amber like that, making her feel bad for no reason over something that we had already planned.

Maya didn't care about me or the casualties of her decisions. That much had been clear years ago and why I was doubting it now was beyond me.

"No, it wasn't you. It had been a long time coming, but she's about to get what's coming to her," I said, brushing past Amber and stalking after Maya.

She wasn't getting away with hurting me again, not this time. I was doing what I should have done years ago and following her. We were going to hash this out if it killed me. I was done watching her walk away.

CHAPTER 45

As we stood on our marks, waiting for the scene to unfold around us, I felt Maya's hand brush over my shoulder with a familiarity that made me smile. She leaned closer, breaking character for a moment to whisper in my ear, "My house tonight?"

I tried to ignore the flutter of my heart; we were friends. Best friends, but just friends. She didn't mean it like that, and despite the butterflies I was feeling, I didn't want her to mean it like that. Did I? Neither of us were straight, but that didn't mean I wanted her. Even if I maybe felt a little something more than friendship for her, it didn't matter. I didn't want to risk our friendship; she was too important to me. It was getting harder to ignore, though, especially with her playful gestures and harmless flirting. I struggled to remind myself that she did it with everyone. It didn't mean anything. She was just a damned good actress and a better friend.

There wasn't anything I wouldn't do for her and I wouldn't lose that for anything.

I wanted to agree. I loved going to her house and being around her Gram and little Leslie, but I couldn't.

I had a meeting with some execs right after we wrapped for the day and I had no idea how long it would take, nor what it was about. I was starting to get nervous and thought about telling her how nervous I was, but I didn't want to burden her with that. After all, it was probably nothing important. It wasn't the first time they'd kept me after shooting for something trivial and probably wouldn't be the last.

"Can't," I whispered back, apologetic. "Bronson's keeping me after."

"Detention?" she asked with a teasing, low laugh.

"Might as well be," I said, grinning.

Before either of us could say anything else, the scene begun, and we both slipped into our roles.

CHAPTER 46

I knew it was foolish to wait around for her, but I had nothing better to do. At least that was what I was telling myself. It wasn't that I didn't want to be without her and her glowing smile. It wasn't that I was an idiot who was falling for her best friend. I was just being a good friend. As much as Sav had tried to hide it, I knew she was nervous about the meeting. Besides, Bronson was a bit of creep and I wanted to be here to rescue her if he tried for some one-on-one time with her after the meeting. I didn't think he would, not really, but the older girls were always warning us to be careful around him and I didn't take that lightly.

I hoped the meeting was nothing, but I had a nagging feeling she was right to be worried, so I stuck around. I went over to craft services for a snack to kill some time and was happy to run into Lauren. She was in her twenties with curly blonde hair and a friendly smile. She played Savannah's older sister and was always a welcome face as far as I was concerned.

"How's it going, kid?" she asked, patting me on the back while reaching around me to grab the chocolate tart she knew I had been eyeing.

I rolled my eyes at her. I was seventeen, hardly a kid, and she wasn't that much older. I was about to say so when she grinned and handed the tart to me.

I smiled and raised it in toast to her before taking a mouthwatering bite. It was every bit as delicious as always and I couldn't get enough.

A moan slipped out of my mouth that made Lauren laugh before saying, "Quit making a scene. What are you still doing here, anyway?"

I took another bite, moaning more dramatically and louder.

"Ugh, actresses," she said in mock disgust.

We both laughed at that before she said again, "But really, kiddo, don't you have homework to be doing or something?"

As much as I hated the way she said it, she wasn't wrong. I was finishing out my last year of tutoring before I would finally be considered a high school graduate. I had thought about dropping out like a lot of other working kids my age had done. After all, I had found my calling in acting. It wasn't like I was going to need to do complex equations or dissect the works of Plato and Aristotle in the future. I would have dropped out already if it hadn't been for Sav. She placed so much importance on getting a good education, and being her study buddy gave me a great excuse to spend even more time with her. Besides, if she didn't kill me for dropping out, I knew disappointing her would do me in.

"Sav had to stay late. I'm hopeless at studying without her."

She nodded. "That's right. I heard some studio execs were rounding her up. Heard they're looking for a singer."

"What for?" I asked, curious and confused. We all sang. You didn't get a spot at Hollywood High or a part in the show without being able to carry a tune. We were all good, but I would be the first to admit that Savannah was great. It was no secret she was the best of us. I supposed it made sense that if they needed a singer, they would go to her.

She looked around and the sudden seriousness in her face had me worried, especially when she said, "I really shouldn't say."

"Come on; Sav'll tell me the second she's out, anyway. What'd you hear?"

She lowered her voice, saying, "Between me and you, I've been looking for other work."

I gasped. "You're leaving the show? You can't!"

She shushed me and said lower and slower, "You don't understand. I'm saying I have been looking and that if I were you, I would be, too."

Shit.

This job was all I had. It was my life. "You can't be serious."

She frowned. "It makes sense. You guys aren't getting any younger. Either they were going to have to follow you lot to college or careers, or the show was going to end."

It made sense, and I hated that I had been naive enough to not have seen the end coming.

"Sav's gonna be devastated," I said.

Lauren shook her head. "Sav'll be fine. She's the star. They already have something lined up for her after this. Why do you think they're looking for a singer? Why else would they be meeting with her? She's been telling me for ages that she's ready to move on and focus on her music career. I'd be surprised if she didn't ask for this. She's been looking for an end to this."

That couldn't be true. She couldn't have started this. She knew how important the show was to me, and it was important to her, too, right? She wouldn't have asked for its end. She couldn't have, but the more I thought about it, the more pieces fell into place.

She had been getting antsier with shootings lately, continually mentioning how much she loved singing and wished the show was more singing and less acting. I hadn't paid much attention to that, but now it felt like I was a fool for not having seen it sooner. Now it seemed like her dream was coming at my expense and I couldn't believe she would do that to me.

I was livid. I left Lauren where she was standing and took off toward the conference rooms.

Chapter 47

I couldn't believe what I was hearing. I hadn't known what to expect, but if I had had a million guesses, this wouldn't have even made the list.

"You're joking. What about the others?"

Bronson smiled. "It's show biz. They'll understand, and if anyone should get that, it would be you, Hollywood," he said, chuckling, but I didn't feel any warmth coming from him. It was starting to feel like this wasn't an option and was already a foregone conclusion.

I was torn, and I hated that. I had been thinking for a long while now about breaking away from the show to get into singing for real, dreaming about it, and now that the opportunity was in front of me, I felt ungrateful. In my dreams, I hadn't thought for a second that the show wouldn't continue without me if I left. I assumed they would just write me out and keep going, but, apparently, that wasn't the plan.

"They'll get other jobs. Don't worry about them. Any one of them in your same position would jump at the chance."

Thinking about my castmates that had become a second family to me, I knew he was wrong. Not that they weren't talented and would get their own jobs, they would, but I couldn't imagine any of them being willing to jump ship knowing they were signing the dismissal of everyone else. Maya wouldn't do that to me, and I already knew I would hate myself if I did that to her. The show was everything to her. I couldn't take that away from her, but I wasn't sure I had much of a choice. I still had to try, though, but I didn't want to make this about her. I knew that wasn't an argument that would win Bronson over, so instead I said, "What about the show? The fans?"

Bronson looked back and forth between the team, and his smile dropped completely. "I don't think you understand, Savannah. The contract you signed means we own you. This meeting was more of a curtesy than anything, but this is what you're going to be doing. That is, if you want to keep working in the industry."

Shit. The threat had been implied, but I didn't think he'd have the nerve to make it known. This was worse than I thought.

"There's nothing you can do about the show? What about writing me off?"

He shook his head. "Honey, you are the show. Hollywood High without Savannah Hollywood is just another high school, not worth anyone's time."

"Maya could replace me," I said, grasping at straws now.

"She doesn't have half your talent. This show will be her last if I have anything to say about it."

I knew Bronson didn't really like Maya. The feeling was mutual. Neither of us liked or trusted the man, but I was better at hiding my distrust and disdain. I was surprised he was being open about not liking Maya, though. My heart sank and my brain raced, trying to find a way out of this, trying to find a way to fix things, but I couldn't see a way out. I knew Maya didn't like singing nearly as much as she did acting, but maybe she would consider coming with me.

"I'll do it," I breathed, out and saw the powerful suited men around me grin before I interjected, "on one condition."

Bronson's grin faded, and he looked at me condescendingly before saying, "Sweetheart, I don't think you understand how little power you have here."

I smiled sweetly at him, saying, "Oh sweetie, I understand exactly how much power I have here. As you've very clearly said, I'm the star here, and me not cooperating with my new career path would make a lot of people's lives a lot harder. Besides, it's an easy condition." Here goes nothing. "Maya and I are a package deal. If you want me, she comes, too. She's good, a better actress, but a damn good singer and I won't sing one damned note without her. You can make me stand on whatever stage you want, but you can't make me sing."

The men looked at Bronson nervously; he glared at me. "Fine, be a little brat. I always knew you were a diva. We'll find some way to fit her in."

I genuinely grinned at that.

"Do we have a deal?" he asked.

I knew it wasn't really a question, but I was happy I could at least save Maya.

I heard the door whoosh open, but he already had my hand grasped in his, his eyes trained on me, the threat implicit in them. I didn't dare look away.

Seeing the challenge in his eyes and not willing to back down, I kept smiling and said, "We have a deal."

I heard a gasp and looked over and saw Maya. My smile fell when I registered the betrayal on her face. It took me a minute to realize how this might look.

I pulled my hand away quickly, feeling guilty.

"My," I said carefully, "I have some news."

"I can't believe it," she breathed out. "You're actually abandoning us."

"It's not like that," I said.

Bronson and his shit-eating grin chimed in, "You should be happy for her. When she approached us about going solo, we knew we had to take her up on it."

My jaw dropped. That lying weasel. "That's not what-" I started, but the words died in my throat at seeing the raw pain on her face, and my own pain multiplied when I saw the hurt turn to anger.

"Good riddance. The show needed a new star, any-way. I could take her place."

I bristled at that. It didn't matter that I had made the same suggestion a few minutes ago, it killed me that she was so quick to believe them and so quick to dismiss and try to replace me.

"Unfortunately, no can do," Bronson said. "The fans wouldn't go for it. The show lives and dies with Savan-nah Hollywood, and she just signed its death warrant, but we'll put in a good word for you with the other studios."

She wouldn't even look at me, but the hope on her face at his statement made me even more nauseous.

"Come with me!" I blurted out.

She leveled a glare at me. "And what? Be your assis-tant?"

"Sing with me," I corrected.

She was looking at me like I was beneath her, like if she could she would crush me beneath her shoe. "I would never lower myself to be your backup singer. I'd rather never work again."

With that, she turned on her heel and walked out. I watched her go, feeling frozen, feeling my heart break, feeling the finality of the moment.

I knew instinctively I was seeing the last of Maya Ryder.

CHAPTER 48

PRESENT DAY ~ MAYA

It was impossible not to think about the similarities of tonight with thirteen years ago. Here I was, walking away from her again. I should have known better than to trust her, should've known better than to get close to her, closer than I ever had been. I shouldn't have been naive enough to give her the power to hurt me again.

Fool me once, shame on her, fool me twice, shame on me. I was the fool.

I knew from experience she wouldn't chase me, so I didn't rush. Despite our earlier plan, I wasn't trying to make more of a scene than I needed to.

Once I was out of her sight, I slowed to a stroll, letting myself breathe and feel the night air on my face, letting myself cool down.

I thought I would be feeling more than I was, but I was just tired, numb.

I took out my phone to call a cab. No more limos for me, but before I could dial, I felt a hand on my shoulder. I startled, turning around quickly and feeling my heart jump into my throat. Savannah was standing there. She had followed me; she had actually chased after me. It didn't matter to me how pissed she looked right now, I felt most of my earlier hostility drain out of me seeing her standing there. She had chased after me.

Maybe she was different after all. Maybe she wasn't the same girl that ruined my life way back then. It was possible, and I owed it to my heart to find out. We were too old to live with regrets.

"What the actual fuck, Ryder?" Sav bit out, and I had to stop myself from taking a step toward her, from pulling her mouth to mine. Hearing my last name come out of her mouth like that, seeing how hot she was when she was angry made me want her even more, but I stayed back giving her her distance. If she wanted to actually do this here and now, I was down.

"Are you sure you want to do this here?"

She glared at me. "I'm sure you have some explaining to do. What the fuck was that with Amber? She didn't have anything to do with this."

I felt a flicker of irritation. Of course she would bring up Amber first. Of the long list of things we should be talking about Amber didn't even make the list.

"Of course she's the first thing you want to talk about," I said under my breath.

"What the hell is that supposed to mean?" She spat at me. "You're the one that attacked her. Of course I want to figure out what the hell that was about."

"You wouldn't get it," I said, taking a step back. I didn't know if I could do this after all, admit to her how seeing Amber with her made me feel.

Some of that must have shown on my face because she softened, and then, as if reflexively trying to correct that, she folded her arms. "I mean it's not like you, not really. With anyone except me anyway, so yeah, I think you owe me an explanation."

"Look, I was waiting for you so we could get this over with, and you were late. You left me waiting and then when I finally found you, you were busy talking to my replacement, so yeah, I felt some kind of fucking way about it, Sav."

Sav dropped her arms, and her eyes widened. She swayed like she was going to take a step forward, but then thought better of it. "Your replacement?" she asked.

"The second you threw me away, threw away Hollywood High, you didn't waste any time replacing me with her. It was like I didn't mean anything to you, and here you are doing it again. Although this time you were clever enough to have everything neatly tied up in your little contract. Nothing messy about it; a legally binding clean break."

"I-" she started, emotions flashing over her face quicker than I could register them, before she closed her eyes and took a deep breath. When she opened them, disbelief reigned. "Do you want to start with the past or now? Cause it's about time we hashed this out."

I just crossed my arms and waited.

"Fine," she said. "We'll start back then and work our way forward so you can see what a giant jerk you're being. Thirteen years ago, when I was 17, I walked into a boardroom full of industry execs who already had their minds made up that the show was over. I had signed my life away to be on the show. You know that, you signed the same contract."

I begrudgingly had to nod, conceding. She was right; that contract had been no joke.

"So, they pulled me in there, a seventeen-year-old kid without a lawyer, without a legal guardian, without anyone looking out for me, and told me they owned me and were going to make me a star. It didn't matter to them that I wanted to keep going with the show. They saw me as more lucrative as a singer. I tried to tell them the show could go on with or without me, hell I even said you should be the new lead, but they wouldn't listen."

She couldn't mean that. There was no way in hell she suggested I take over for her. She couldn't have.

"There's no way," I said, shaking my head. "If that were true, you would've told me, and Bronson said it was your idea."

"Bronson's a conniving bastard and you know it. I couldn't do shit about it. Miraculously, I got him to agree to letting you sing with me, if you wanted to. It was my one condition, that you had to have the choice to sing with me, but you didn't give me the chance to tell you. Bronson saw a way out and lied his ass off. I wanted to follow you out, but from the look you gave me, I knew you wouldn't have listened. Your mind was made up."

I thought back to that day and had to concede again that she was right. I had been so angry with her for all these years, for throwing away our friendship, for letting me go so easily and not following me out, but if I was being honest with myself, she was right. Her following me wouldn't have changed a thing. I would have believed Bronson over her, an unforgiveable fact.

"I'm sorry," I breathed out.

She blinked, surprised. "What?" she asked. Her expression betraying a mix of confusion and hopefulness.

"I said I'm sorry. I was hurt and angry, but I should have given you a chance. You were my best friend and I should have listened to you over him. I shouldn't have questioned you. I hate that I was so ready to see the worst in you, and I'm sorry."

"I-" she started, "um," she was floundering before she landed on, "thank you."

I nodded, looking at my shoes and then at the sidewalk, and the cars on the street, anywhere but her eyes. "In the spirit of honesty and rewriting history, I'm sorry about tonight, too. I was more of a jerk than I had the right to be. Seeing you all cozy with Amber brought me right back there. I hated myself for it, but it was hard seeing all the pictures of the two of you posted everywhere when we stopped talking, seeing the shiny new popstar friend you replaced me with."

"I didn't-" she started, but I waved her off.

"I know you didn't replace me. I shut you out. I know that now but I told myself that even though I blocked you, even though I went out of my way to not be anywhere near you, that if you had wanted to, you would have reached out."

"I felt like you hated me and wanted space. It killed me, but I was trying to be respectful of that, to give you the space you wanted."

"I thought I wanted it, but I was young and stupid. I didn't want space. I wanted you."

"I didn't want to lose your friendship, either."

I sighed and made what I knew would be a life-changing decision to stop caring about the consequences, to stop lying to myself. Even if she didn't feel the same, she deserved to know how deeply I had fallen for her, how wrapped around her finger I was. Whether or not she wanted me, despite the fact that she was going to reject me, had even tried to let me down easy earlier tonight, I had to tell her.

I slowly shook my head, finally looking her in the eye. I took a step forward, closing the gap between us as I said, "No, Sav, you're not listening. I *wanted* you."

I closed the gap and kissed her hard. Her lips came alive against mine and I felt her hands pulling at my neck, fingers lacing in my hair, pulling me closer. I smiled against her lips and pulled away.

"Correction," I said, grinning down at her. She was smiling and breathless and I had never seen a more beautiful sight. "I *want* you. Nothing past tense about it."

She looked unsure for a moment. "All this time?"

"I never stopped."

"Good," she said, grinning again and pulling me to her. I gasped at the feel of her lips against mine again. I didn't think I'd be that lucky again. I felt her tongue slip into my parted mouth and I groaned against her. I wanted this, desperately, but my mind was racing a mile a minute and she was too damned distracting.

I pulled away quickly. "I need a minute," I said apologetically. "What changed between now and earlier today?" I asked, needing to hear her say it, needing to know why she wasn't rejecting me, needing to know how she felt. Was I just a pretty pair of lips to her? If I was, could I be okay with that? I wasn't sure.

"I could ask you the same," she said, watching me.

I shook my head. "No, you were going to let me down easy earlier. What changed your mind?"

She rapidly blinked. "I was what? When?" she asked.

I couldn't believe her mind was so clouded she couldn't remember earlier. "In the car on the ride over here, you looked at me with pity and said my nickname. You were going to tell me you enjoyed your time with me but that you were relieved for it to be over. I couldn't bear to hear you say it, so I didn't let you."

She looked at me, really looked at me, before breaking into a grin. "You really are so dense," she said, laughing.

I felt my eyebrows pull together in a frown, but she held up her hand.

"I was going to tell you that contract be damned, I wanted you. The only thing I was sick of was the lying, to everyone, and to myself. I want to do this."

My heart was pounding out of my chest and I felt my hopes soar, but I needed clarification. "You want to do this for real?"

She nodded. "You've been a great fake girlfriend, but I want you for real, nothing fake about it."

I couldn't believe my ears. I was the luckiest girl in the world, and I knew it. I pulled her in tight, knowing I never wanted to let go.

CHAPTER 49

MAYA

Waking up in the bed we had been sharing, with Sav cuddled up next to me, for the first time, I could just enjoy it. I didn't have to overthink, and it was nice. I still couldn't believe she was mine, and that I had wasted so much time and energy being stubborn. If I had just given her a chance, listened to her sooner, I would've been much happier. I vowed to myself to not make that mistake again. She was mine and I was hers, and I'd make sure to do everything I could to keep it that way.

She stirred, and I watched a sleepy smile settle over her face as she blinked up at me. I smiled back at her, smoothing her unruly hair away from her face.

"This feels like a dream," she said, musing. "If it is, please don't wake me up."

"Better than a dream," I said, pulling her closer to me and kissing the top of her head. "I can't believe we were so clueless for so long."

She laughed at that. "Speak for yourself."

I looked at her pointedly. "Only one of us was married before and it wasn't me."

"Ughh," she groaned. "Don't remind me, but yes, fine, we were both clueless." She interlaced her fingers with mine and squeezed. "At least we have each other now. Nothing fake about it."

"Definitely, although that reminds me, you're going to have to tell Elite I didn't violate my contract."

She burst into laughter at that. "Deal. I'll tell them I was begging for this," I laughed at that, and as her lips moved down my body, she breathed out, "and today I'll have you begging."

This wasn't how things normally went for me, but I was surprised to find I wasn't minding letting Sav take the lead for once. When her lips found their way to my inner thigh, I knew nothing could feel sweeter.

I was in heaven and could certainly get used to this.

HOLLYWOOD'S HOOKUP TURNED DUET PARTNER

Last night was monumental for Savannah Hollywood, the opening night of her world tour, and she wasn't alone. Hollywood and her latest beau, Maya Ryder, have taken the world by storm stealing the hearts of all Savannah's adoring fans. Many are saying it's the happiest they've ever seen her.

The screams were deafening when she introduced her special guest and they treated the audience to a beautiful duet. There wasn't a dry eye in the stadium when the girls were done.

The stadium went wild when Maya pulled Savannah to her, dipped her, and kissed her. One thing is for certain, Hollywood is smitten and her fans are loving it. As Hollywood's legal team prepares for her upcoming day in court, Hollywood has made it clear that Maya is here to stay. With Darren's acting career declining and Maya's overnight rise to stardom, it's become clear that Darren has lost that Hollywood magic that made him a star, or maybe he just lost Hollywood.

Darren Dawson's Devastating Day in Court

Hollywood's legal team decimated Darren's joke of a counsel in court. This reporter has been told that Darren had been requesting spousal support to "maintain the lifestyle he had grown accustomed to" while married to Hollywood. What I wouldn't have given to be a fly on the wall in that courtroom when the judge heard that.

Darren isn't by any means destitute, but he stood to lose a lot in the divorce since Savannah's net worth is over five times his at the latest estimates.

However, rumor has it, he was laughed out of court when he tried to go for an additional million for "pain and suffering" caused by her cheating on him. If he had any evidence, we haven't seen it, but Savannah's legal team definitely didn't show up empty-handed. They had receipts and proof of no less than twenty different women he was having extramarital relations with, the most noteworthy being entertainment reporter Teresa Terrence from her self-titled show Teresa Talks.

Hollywood left triumphant on the arm of her beau Maya Ryder. When reached out to for a comment, Hollywood said she is, "Incredibly thankful to all my fans for sticking with me through this difficult and trying time and for being supportive of me being openly queer and openly myself. I appreciate each and every one of you."

Darren hasn't been seen since exiting the courtroom in a hurry having a loud shouting match with his lawyer. We reached out to his team for a comment and were told he had nothing to say.

Savannah Hollywood's Phoenix Rising Records Helps Queer Artists Rise to New Heights

Now that Savannah's divorce is behind her, it seems she's turned her sites to a new project. Her latest album Rising From the Ashes: The Rainbow Edition was released under a pseudo record label she called Phoenix Rising Records. Well, it turns out, Savannah had bigger plans for the label. She has melded her foundation for queer artists into its own label under the same name. Anonymous sources say that queer artists are lining up to sign on with her and that on the large roster of names she has, a few of them will be familiar.

We know that we'll be watching Savannah and Phoenix Rising Records' socials closely for any news about upcoming albums. With the divorce, breaking from her record label, being openly bisexual now, and being in love again, we're sure Savannah has a new album in the works and hope we won't have to wait too long.

As for the label, they've announced that they're announcing their artists later this week, and we can't wait to see who's lucky enough to be signed on to her label.

ARE DARREN DAWSON'S HOLLYWOOD DAYS BEHIND HIM? *Darren Dawson's latest movie, A Night to Remember, premiered last night, and can we just say, in addition to having needed a heavy rewrite, it should have been renamed. To say it was a snooze fest is an understatement. Marketed as the horror movie of the summer, the only thing scary about the movie was Darren's acting. How we ever thought that man could act is beyond me, but losing Savannah Hollywood seemed to take away all his charm. Without Hollywood, he's no longer a hotshot in Hollywood.*

Whether or not he'll be signed for anything else remains to be seen, but what isn't up for debate is that the sun seems to be setting quickly on his career while Savannah Hollywood's career is skyrocketing. This reporter thinks it's clear who lucked out with this divorce. Rumor has it Darren's latest starring role has been recast to a younger, more attractive actor. Again, he couldn't be reached for comment.

One thing is clear, Hollywood's future is looking brighter without him in it.

Hollywood's In her Heyday

Ladies and gentlemen, Savannah Hollywood has finally done it. She won her day in court and is officially the hottest divorcee in Hollywood. Just when we were thinking she couldn't be more impressing, last night she took home, not one, not two, but three Grammys.

She looked beautiful in a deep emerald off the shoulder satin gown. Her beau Maya Ryder was a sight for sore eyes in a midnight blue gown and was beaming with pride at showing Savannah off. You could practically see the love in the air between those two. The only thing missing were diamonds on their left hands, but this reporter is sure it won't be long. With the way those two look at each other with such longing, it's clear wedding bells are in the air.

THE END

So, what did you think of Becoming A Bi-con?

I would love to hear any and all of your thoughts! If you would be so kind as to leave any review it would be greatly appreciated. Any review, good or bad, short or long, is always welcome.

For updates on my next book or to tell me what you thought about this one, you can find me:

Visit my website:
Thelibraryofsarahzane.com

Or follow me on TikTok or Instagram:
@LibraryofSarahZane

Or my Facebook page: AuthorSarah Zane

Please come find me on any of those platforms, I would love to hear what you thought about my book!

About The Author

 Sarah is an author of happy endings for traumatized queers.

She is a bisexual feminist and a licensed therapist. Her stories deal with themes of feminism, trauma, sexuality, and mental health.

She lives in New England with her 2 black cats named Gatsby and Mr. Darcy. When she isn't writing, she can be found perusing a book in her home library, making chaotic book themed videos for TikTok (aka Booktok), taking forest walks, visiting castles, planning exotic trips she can't afford, or cuddled up with one of her cats crying over fictional characters yelling at them about how badly they need therapy.

For more from Sarah Zane, check out...

Beautiful Little Fool.
A sapphic, feminist retelling of the Great Gatsby from Daisy's POV.
Sequel coming December 2024...

Off Script: A Book Ball Fantasy Adventure
A fantasy adventure story about Sadie, a fantasy author whose first convention goes haywire when her characters literally jump off the page.

Cosplay and Confrontation
A sapphic rivals-to-lovers cosplayers romcom that takes place at the same fantasy convention in Off Script.

Under Lock and Key
A sapphic cozy fantasy retelling of Bluebeard about a blue-haired temptress innkeeper and the mysterious woman who wanders into her inn and falls for her charms.

Acknowledgements

Firstly, I have to thank my mom, without whom this book wouldn't exist. As much as I hope you don't read parts of this book (the spicy ones), it only exists because of how much you helped me through my divorce. Without your help and support, I doubt I could have been half as brave as I was. You were there for me when I needed you and you're the reason I'm much happier now. Thank you for being modern enough to support me leaving a marriage that was killing me slowly.

To my Book Babes of MA, thank you for encouraging me to publish spicy scenes that otherwise might not have seen the light of day. Thank you guys for helping me make the story was it is today.

To Stella, thank you for bringing my beautiful girls to life with this gorgeous cover. I loved you already, but I love you eternally now, you're stuck with me.

To the Elite Connections anthology crew, thank you all so much for this really fun prompt that turned into this incredibly cathartic story.

To my family and friends, thank you all so much for the love and support. It means more to me than I can express. There are way too many of you to list here, but know I appreciate you.

Thank you to my beloved Booktok community of wonderful authors, readers, and new friends. I have so much love for you all and am incredibly happy to have found such a great community that makes me feel so at home.

Last but not least, thank you to you, dear reader, for reading this and helping support my crazy dream of being an author.

From the bottom of my heart, I love you all.